CRISS CROSS

PsyCop 2

CRISS CROSS

— a PSYCOP novella —

Jordan Castillo Price

PsyCop 2

jCPBOOKS.com

Standalone print edition published in the
United States in 2016 by JCP Books
www.jcpbooks.com

First Standalone Print Edition

ISBN-13 978-1-935540-87-8

Cover art by Jordan Castillo Price

Audio edition available

Chapter 1

It was a pretty good day, for October in Chicago. The weather was warm enough that I could get away with wearing just jeans, a T-shirt, a flannel shirt, and my threadbare jean jacket. I could see my breath as we set the rowboat in the water, Maurice in his knee-high rubber boots, steadying the small aluminum boat so I could climb in. Water squished through my black Converse high-tops. Not the best shoes to wear fishing, I gathered.

But I'd never been fishing before, so how the hell would I know?

Maurice heaved himself over the side, thrust an oar into the slimy green water on the bank of the Calumet, and shoved off. And he did it with an ease that reminded me that even though he was graying, he was still in reasonably good shape.

Maurice Taylor had been my partner in the PsyCop Unit for a dozen years, and now he was retired. We'd been quintessential opposites when the force had matched us up: him, a mature black man without a lick of psychic ability, who'd inched his way up to detective with years of hard, honest police work. And me, an impulsive white kid with no friends, whose sixth sense was always tuned to eleven unless I was on an anti-psyactive drug cocktail.

Maurice was still old. And he still had his common sense, far as I could tell. Me? I wasn't a kid anymore, but at least I'd managed to make a few friends. Other than that, I couldn't really vouch for myself.

"Give that oar over here," Maurice said, stretching his hand out to me. "We be goin' in circles all day, if I let you just splash it all over the place like that."

I didn't argue. Maurice is more stubborn than I am. I know this.

Maurice took several deep breaths as he rowed us farther from shore. The Calumet's current wasn't particularly fast in the fall. It had pockets of reedy marsh along the banks that seemed like ideal places to just sit in your boat and while away the day. A train clanged by to the north of us and the scream of a siren drifted by from a stretch of elevated highway. Nature.

"Smell that fine air," Maurice said.

I grunted. It smelled like algae and exhaust fumes to me.

Maurice pulled a few more strokes with the oars and then eased our anchor—a hunk of metal that'd been part of a barbell in another existence—over the side.

"Shouldn't I have, uh...a lifejacket on?"

Maurice smiled and started fiddling with his rod. Or reel. Or whatever the fishing pole thing is called. "S'okay, Victor. Water ain't but waist high."

I glanced over the side of the boat. The water was opaque green. Hard to tell if Maurice was exaggerating.

He put the fishing pole in my hand and pulled out another. "Just set there and wait until I show you how to cast. Else you'll tear your eye out with the hook."

I looked down at the hook. Maurice had squished a worm onto it. A worm spirit didn't appear and immediately start telling me about the moment of its death, so I presumed I was safe from the spirits of bugs. But then it moved and I realized it was still alive. Gross.

Maurice cast his own line with a fairly straightforward explanation of what he was doing, then exchanged it with me for the first fishing pole, which he also cast.

I stared out at the little red floaty things that marked where our hooks had sunk and waited for more instructions.

Maurice wedged his fishing pole into a groove on the floor of the boat and unzipped his duffel bag. He pulled out a thermos and a battered plastic travel mug.

"What next?" I asked him.

Maurice poured some coffee into the mug and handed it to me. The early morning sunlight filtered through the steam that curled up from the surface of the coffee, and I felt like the two of us were in a Folgers commercial. Maurice poured another cup for himself, screwed the stopper back onto the thermos, and sighed. "We wait," he said.

I noticed he was smiling, a soft, kind of distant smile as he gazed out over the water, conveniently ignoring the beer cans and plastic shopping bags that floated around us. Retirement suited him.

We drank our coffees together in silence, and we stared at the water while I tried to control the shivering, me sitting there in wet canvas sneakers in October. It was warm for October, but not that warm. I wedged my fishing pole into the groove in the floor as I'd seen Maurice do and poured myself another coffee. I contemplated pouring out the rest of the contents of the thermos onto my freezing cold feet, but I figured it would only feel good for about a minute, and then the coffee would cool and pretty soon my feet would just be wet again. I saved the coffee for drinking, instead.

"So," Maurice said, after he finished his coffee. "Warwick find you a new partner yet?

"Yeah, a couple days ago. Some guy. His name's Roger Burke."

I really couldn't think of much to say about Detective "please, call me Roger," Burke. He was kinda like white bread. When I was a teenager, I would have been pretty eager to get him down my throat. But now that I was looking at forty, I found him a little bland.

Don't get me wrong, Roger was cute. He had a ready smile that he lavished on me at the drop of a hat. His thick hair was naturally blond, cut short and smart. His eyebrows and eyelashes were a darker blond, framing greenish hazel eyes.

I'd never seen him in anything less than a sport coat, but judging by the way it sat on his shoulders and buttoned smoothly over his nipped waist, I was guessing he probably exercised regularly, and was hiding a set of washboard abs under his perfectly pressed dress shirt.

It was difficult to say if he'd pitch for my team or not. Once upon a time I assumed that all the other cops except for me were straight. That was before Detective Jacob Marks cornered me in the bathroom at Maurice's retirement party.

I was still too fixated on Jacob to really give a damn if Roger Burke slept with men, women, or inflatable farm animals, for that matter.

"What's this Burke guy like?" Maurice asked.

I decided it would be far too gay to tell Maurice what color Roger Burke's eyes were. And besides, Maurice wouldn't give a shit. "He always buys the coffee. Seems decent enough. He was a detective for five years in Buffalo."

"New York?"

"Yeah."

"Huh." The plastic floaty on Maurice's line dipped beneath the water. He reeled the line in carefully but all that was on the hook was a drowned worm. He cast it back out. "What about that Mexican girl?"

"That Mexican girl" was Lisa Gutierrez. She'd been selected to be my non-psychic partner, or Stiff, after Maurice retired. Things had worked well between us, until our sergeant figured out that she was a psychic herself. She'd rigged her test scores to get the job.

"She's in California at some place called PsyTrain. Even if she decides to come back here once she's done, they'd never pair us up. They'd need to put her with a Stiff."

"Too bad. Heard the two of you hit it off."

I froze, and not just because ice crystals were forming on my sneakers. I'd been wondering if we'd have this conversation, just me, Maurice and a bunch of garbage floating around in the Calumet River. The little talk where I told him I liked men.

"We, uh…. She's nice."

Maurice reeled his line in a couple of turns and gazed out over the river. He didn't say anything more. I let my breath out slowly, relieved that I'd dodged the bullet, but maybe a little disappointed, too. A few moments of really, really awkward conversation, and then he'd probably never mention it again.

Heck, according to Jacob, Maurice probably already knew. Or at least suspected. Twelve years and no girlfriend? That might be significant if we were talking about an average guy—but it was *me* under the microscope. For all Maurice knew, I was just too messed up to have a woman in my life. I was probably too messed up to have a man in my life too, come to think of it. But since Jacob was a big, strong man with a gun, a cop who knew how to kick ass and take names, I figured he could hold his own.

The two cups of coffee I'd just sucked down roiled around in my stomach, and I hung my head over the side of the boat and tried to talk myself out of being sick. I'd swallowed a donut in three bites on my way out the door, but it wasn't doing a very good job of soaking anything up. Acid licked at the back of my throat and I swallowed hard.

"Don't tell me you're seasick," Maurice said, his eyes still focused on the floaties a few dozen yards away as if I wasn't turning green and gulping air.

I seized on the chance to blame my nausea on anything other than my own internal freak-out. "Maybe," I said. "Haven't been on a boat since I went on that horrible cruise when I turned thirty."

I stared down at the soupy green water sloshing against the side of the rowboat, and picked out tiny round shapes that were plants, or snails, or some other mysterious bits of life in the murk.

"Just set there," Maurice said. "It'll pass."

A larger pale, round shape floated beneath the murky water, probably a shopping bag, or maybe a milk jug. I tried to distract myself by imagining a homie out drinking milk with his posse and chucking the plastic bottle into the river, but I didn't find my own humor particularly entertaining.

It bothered me, not being able to tell what the thing was, and I leaned my face closer to the water and squinted at it. I noticed there was another one, about the same size and shape but maybe a little farther down, to my right. And another to my left. My vision seemed to open up and I realized these pale shapes were all around us, like cloud formations beneath the river's surface.

Some kind of algae, then. Or maybe even pale, sandy mounds, with the Calumet's bottom as close as Maurice had said it was, even closer, us bobbing in a couple of feet of water where we just could have waded instead, if I were dressed appropriately.

I pushed myself up on the side of the boat as my nausea receded. I was just about to ask Maurice about his trip to Fort Lauderdale when the underwater shape surged up toward me and coalesced into a pale, dead face.

I snapped up tall and the fishing pole leapt out of my grip. I managed to grab it before it fell into the water, but maybe I should've just let it drop. Maybe I wouldn't have looked like I was shaking so hard if I didn't have a big, telltale fishing line visibly quivering between me and the water.

The water that was full of dead people.

Maurice stared at me for a beat, glanced over the side, then took the fishing pole from my hands and wedged it into the bottom of the boat. "What you see?" he said calmly.

I knew what I must look like, whites of my eyes showing all around, face paler than usual. The Look. The one that said I'd just seen something. Maurice knew The Look.

I closed my eyes and images of pallid, distended faces bobbing to the surface filled my memory. Hundreds of them, eyes open and unseeing, a landscape of them stretching to the horizon—or at least the highway.

There wouldn't be that many there. Not in real life. It was just my own mind fucking with me.

"It bad?" Maurice said gently.

I opened my eyes and stared hard at his brown, gray-whiskered face. I took another breath. It wasn't that bad, I told myself. I'd just seen a handful of revenants and let my imagination run wild. It wasn't as if I'd never seen dead people before, I told myself. It wasn't like I'd never seen a ghost.

I peeked over the side.

A face peered back at me, rubbery mouth opening and closing like it was trying to talk—but the water didn't move and no bubbles came out. The face next to it blinked. A hand moved toward the surface of the water like a pale, bloated spider, reaching for me. And beyond it, another hand. And another beyond that.

"Jesus," I said. I jerked myself upright and started chafing my arms. "The water's full of them."

Maurice reeled in his drowned worm, and my empty hook, and then the anchor. I felt him shove the oar into the riverbed and give us a push toward shore.

"Should I make some phone calls, have 'em drag it?" Maurice asked.

"I don't know." Was anybody missing? Yeah, probably. But dozens of somebodies? Maybe hundreds? "I just...." I sighed and made a "whatever" gesture. "I don't know."

CHAPTER 2

I helped Maurice load the boat into the back of his Ford Explorer and told him I was gonna go home, take an Auracel and have a nice, long nap. Actually, I was planning on taking at least three pills. So I lied.

My phone sat folded in the driver's seat and I flipped it open, hoping for a message from Jacob to calm me down. He's got this voice, low and sexy, more of a purr. And it'd be hard to keep dredging up the image of the river full of dead people if he was whispering sweet nothings into my phone.

There were two messages. Message number one: Roger. "Hi, Vic. Sorry to bother you on your day off. I'm settled in to my new place. It's not too far from your apartment, just a few blocks down, across the street from the supermarket. If you want to share a ride or anything, just let me know."

And message number two: Jacob. "Hey. Remember how I said the Governor was probably going to grant a stay of execution on Hugo Cooper? Looks like I was wrong. I've got to go and witness it. So...I'll be home late. Bye."

His voice dropped about an octave when he said "bye," sultry and inviting. It seemed weird to me that he could be so blasé about witnessing an execution, but that was part and parcel of the job. I'd put away plenty of guys who'd ended up on death row, but it was in my contract that I didn't have to watch 'em fry. Normally both the leads have to go. I only got out of it because I was a certified medium, and who knows what I'd see if I had to be present for the moment of death?

I slipped the phone into my pocket and headed back toward my apartment. Jacob and I didn't live together, not exactly. It was just that he was staying with me until he found a house or a condo. I'd killed this soul-eating incubus in his bedroom, and even though every psychic Jacob knew told him there was no trace of the thing left, he still refused to sleep there.

It'd been a few weeks, but since we both knew Jacob was actually looking at places—and because he thought my apartment looked like a hospital room in a charity ward—we'd never begun feeling too domestic together.

I parked my car, took three flights of stairs two at a time, threw open my front door and flipped on the kitchen light. I went through the living room, bedroom and bathroom and did the same, until the whole place incandesced. Everything in the apartment was white, from the cheap landlord-painted walls to the furniture to the bent plastic miniblinds. When my eyes settled on things that were not white, they invariably turned out to be shadows, nothing more. And that was the way I liked it.

I swallowed all three Auracel tablets at once, and sank down on the futon in the living room. And then I remembered: I'd meant to pick up rubbers on the way home, but in a few minutes I'd be flying too high to drive. It wasn't like Jacob had left a big note on the fridge that said "buy condoms" or anything. In fact, he hadn't said a word about taking anything further than blowjobs after the first time we'd spent the whole night together. It seemed like every day I set off with the intention of bringing home the goods, and then totally forgot about it. I thought it was fairly conspicuous that Jacob never picked any up, either. Since he's the poster child for organizational skills, I can only assume he was leaving the timing up to me. I'm not exactly sure how buying condoms—or not—turned into my issue. Maybe because all the issues in our relationship seemed to be my issues.

A woven blanket of Jacob's was draped haphazardly on the plain canvas futon cover, a splash of taupe, burgundy and black that looked far too dark amid all the white. I pulled it up to my face and inhaled. It smelled like Jacob and his condo, old wood and leather, clean man-smells. I liked Jacob. A lot. A whole lot. So what was this mental block I had about the condoms?

As the Auracel started throwing the room into soft focus, I decided that I was making a bigger deal out of the whole condom thing than I needed to. They still sold them at convenience stores, didn't they? I'd just have a little nap in my Jacob-smelling blanket, and when I woke up, I'd walk to the corner store and buy some. Problem solved.

The drugs kicked in and I dozed. My miniblinds developed strips of black between the slats where sunlight had streamed in earlier. Jacob's blanket was twisted around my ribs.

I sat up and looked hard from shadow to shadow. Nothing moved. Satisfied that I was alone, I yawned and rolled a kink out of my neck. Nice way to spend my day off, doped up and asleep. I considered taking up drinking. But not very seriously, since the dead get really bossy when I drink.

And speaking of the dead...I thought of the floating faces in the river and shuddered. My triple dose of Auracel was still holding up, though, and hypothetically my sixth sense had a lid on it for the time being. But I hadn't been on Auracel when I'd seen them, and the images from before kept replaying themselves in my mind. Those faces. Hairless. Lips wormy and too mobile, forming soundless sounds, words. Hands reaching, trying to break the surface....

I grabbed the first thing I could lay my hands on and threw it across the room. You wouldn't think a plastic coaster would put such a big ding in the wall. Damn.

I looked at the clock. A little after nine. The state still does executions at midnight, as if deliberately and methodically killing someone isn't spooky enough as it is. Jacob would be gone until one, one-thirty. I wanted Jacob. I didn't want to be alone with the memory of those bloated bodies.

I called Lisa and got a message on her cell that said she wouldn't be available for the next couple of weeks due to her coursework, but to leave her a message and she'd be back in touch soon. She sounded perky, like she couldn't wait to go meditate, or whatever they were teaching her. Couldn't she have phone hours, I wondered. Did she need to devote so much time to chanting "om" that she couldn't just talk to me for five fucking minutes to reassure me that the river wasn't really full of dead people?

I closed my eyes and breathed carefully, and told myself that I did not want to strangle Lisa. I debated taking another Auracel, but since I had to work the next day, opted for a Seconal to just knock me out instead.

I tuned the living room TV to a station I didn't receive, slumped on the futon, and watched some static.

I think it's a white-noise kind of thing I'm looking for when I go between TV or radio stations. Something generic to shut out the dead. It's not anything they taught me at Heliotrope Station, better known as Camp Hell, the sicko place where I was supposedly being taught to harness my psychic ability. I'd just picked up static-surfing on my own.

Channel 8 was usually pretty good for a gray, textured nothingness. I hit zero-eight on the remote and settled in.

Except Channel 8 seemed to be tuning something in tonight. I wondered why that would be. Maybe another station had boosted its signal, or the hole in the ozone happened to be lining up with some broadcast satellite, or maybe Mercury was retrograde. Damn. I'd liked Channel 8 just the way it was.

I made out a face in the static and tried to match it with a familiar celebrity, without luck. I picked out the contour of a cheek, and an open mouth. A hand fluttered up, five fingers blurring. Sign language? I had no idea. But the Seconal was kicking in, combining with the grogginess brought on by all the Auracel I'd taken earlier, and my eyelids drooped despite the nagging compulsion to make sense of what I was seeing.

I wouldn't say I actually slept, at least not the whole time. Camp Hell called it a hypnogogic state, that window between sleeping and waking. Sometimes when I catch myself in that window I feel extraordinarily clear, like I've been going through the day wearing a pair of dirty, smudged sunglasses and it's just occurred to me to take them off. Other times I just feel like I'm falling.

It was in the middle of one of those sickening falling lurches that I snapped awake, as if I'd been caught. Jacob's face was right in mine, and he held me firmly by the upper arms. "Hey," he said when I woke up.

I cleared my throat. "Hey."

He stared hard into my eyes. "Were you...sleeping?"

I raised an eyebrow. Evidently he didn't think so, since he'd felt the need to grab me like that. "I dunno. Not exactly." I shrugged. He let go of me and settled down in a crouch between my legs, with his elbows resting on my knees. "Sort of dreaming."

"Your eyes were half-open, but they were fixed, not moving."

Oh. That must've been really attractive. Good thing anything paranormal, ugly or not, makes Jacob horny. But still, there had to be a limit somewhere, and I wasn't eager to find it. I wondered if he'd had any luck with househunting. And then I remembered he'd been at an execution all night, and it was probably somewhere in the wee hours of the morning. "I took a sleeping pill," I said as I pushed off the back of the futon. He eased back and stood, and gave me a hand up.

I glimpsed Channel 8 but didn't see any more staticky people. Jacob turned off the television, poking the manual on/off button as we went by. The lights in the bedroom were already on; in fact, all the lights in the apartment were still on. I waited for him in the bedroom doorway while he swung around to flick off the kitchen and bathroom lights. I usually left the kitchen light on all night, since it was far enough away from the bedroom to leave my sleep undisturbed, yet it ensured that I wouldn't awake in total darkness and see...well, I dunno what I might see, but I didn't want to find out. But for the past two weeks with Jacob there, I'd been sleeping with the lights out. All of them.

I didn't move as Jacob approached the bedroom. For someone who made me feel so safe, he sure looked like hell. A deep, vertical scowl line I'd never noticed before was wedged between his dark eyebrows, the laugh lines at the corners of his eyes just looked weary, and his mouth was pressed into a grim set. "Are you okay?" I asked. And I felt a little stupid for taking so long to ask it, but at least I'd figured it out eventually. I'm really not accustomed to having to worry about anyone but myself.

Jacob fit himself into the bedroom doorway with me, one of us backed against each jamb, and propped his wrists on my shoulders. We were both a handful of inches over six feet tall, but his solid mass dwarfed me as he pressed his forehead into mine. "That guy they put down today, Hugo Cooper. He was a monster."

"Yeah," I said, as if I knew it all. Cooper had kidnapped three women. Kept them alive in a hundred-degree attic. He probably wouldn't have murdered them if one hadn't escaped and run for help, which caused him to panic and try to erase the whole thing in a brutal, frenzied massacre.

Those were the basics, but I'm sure Jacob would be able give me every last detail, the location of every scattered body part. I hoped he wouldn't.

"No matter how evil they are," I said, "it fucks with your mind to watch 'em fry."

I felt Jacob's breath, warm, on my cheek. He kissed me, a chaste brush of his lips, and my heartbeat sped. "It was lethal injection." He turned toward the bed, and sighed. "But, yeah. It was no picnic."

The little flutter I'd taken for pleasure felt more like panic as Jacob pulled away from me. Faces in the river, dark house, and Lisa unreachable in Santa Barbara. I slipped around him and got into bed, pulling him down beside me. He didn't respond as quickly and eagerly as usual, but he seemed willing enough.

I pulled Jacob close to me, arms around his neck, and pressed my mouth against his. He's got full lips, normally set in a slightly knowing grin; nothing arrogant, just an I-got-the-joke-five-minutes-ago type of look. He worked his way out of his suitcoat as I clung to him and ran my tongue back and forth over his lower lip. His jacket slid from the bed to the floor and he settled himself against me. I ran my hands down his back, which was hot through the fabric of his shirt everywhere it'd been covered by the coat. I could feel the cut of his muscles, even on his back, and even through that shirt. Jacob works out—religiously, I'd learned since he'd been staying with me. And aside from pumping iron, the man takes a run after work if police business doesn't keep him late. *A run.*

Jacob broke our kiss and narrowed his eyes. "Why are you smiling?"

I realized he'd probably still been thinking about the execution and promptly attempted to look serious, even though I was totally busted. "You make me happy. That's all."

Jacob scowled harder. "I don't trust you when you smile."

I pressed myself more firmly into his chest, and wished my psychic powers could also make our clothes disappear. "Really." I loosened his tie. "I had a lousy day too, and I'm glad to see you."

"You had a lousy day...fishing?"

Boy, nothing got past him. "Let's not talk about it." I stripped his shirt off, then pulled my ratty sweatshirt over my head. I knew the perfect thing to take Jacob's mind off the crap day we'd each had. But of course I'd forgotten the condoms—again—so I'd just have to make do. Not that I've ever known anyone to complain about getting a blowjob.

I pushed Jacob onto his back and got to work on his belt. His expression grew less pensive as he watched me unzip his fly and start tracing the muscles on his abs with my tongue. Maybe he even grinned a little, too. Or at least he'd stopped scowling. I ditched the rest of my clothes fast, then finished stripping Jacob a little more respectfully. He wears expensive tailored suits that don't appreciate being torn off and wadded up on the floor. The Seconal—not exactly a modern sleeping pill, actually a barbiturate that used to be a party drug in the seventies—had made me mellow, more apt to finesse his clothes off than tear at them.

Once I'd undressed Jacob I ran my palms down his thighs, feeling the swell of hard muscle beneath the skin. He lay back and watched me taking him in, and he definitely looked less stressed than he had when he'd gotten home. I always thought of him as fearless, but maybe I made him feel safe somehow, too.

I settled myself between his legs with my feet sticking off the bottom of the bed and I kissed him on the stomach again, but now Jacob's cock was brushing against my chest and I let that contact happen, almost as if it was accidental, and felt him swell against me.

I slid my hands over Jacob's hips and held onto them as I worked my mouth lower. His skin was pleasantly salty; the hair on his thighs was soft against my cheek. My mouth found its way to the base of Jacob's cock, and he let out a low groan. His hands covered mine, and our fingers meshed together. He squeezed my fingers encouragingly.

I ran my tongue higher, licking along the underside of his cock while it rose up to meet my mouth. It's a big, wide cock, but it looks right on him. And there's something dirty about trying to cram it into my mouth and going to work the next day with an aching jaw that really gets me off.

"Mmm, yeah."

Speaking of dirty: Jacob's a talker. And keeping my mouth full of cock has the added bonus of me not having to answer him. Not that the words aren't sexy as hell—I just worry that I'll sound like an idiot if I'm the one saying them.

"Uhn, that's right, Vic. Yeah...sweet mouth."

My cock gave a throb into the bedspread, but I couldn't grab it since Jacob was holding my hands tight. The thought of that made me even harder. I got his cockhead into my mouth, and the slick salt of precome touched the back of my tongue.

Jacob gave a sharp gasp and squeezed my fingers.

I felt the girth of him with my lips and slid back, wetting Jacob's cock so it'd slide a little easier.

"God, Vic. Yeah."

I bore down on it on that first good stroke so I took him all the way into my throat. I could appreciate why Seconal was so popular if it made me that relaxed and still let me get hard.

Jacob moaned louder.

I was digging the thought of a big slab of cockmeat invading my throat—probably that was the residual high of the Auracel talking—so I did Jacob hard and fast. Lots of suction, lots of speed. His hands clenched hard at my fingers and his body arched up off the bed.

"Oh God! Oh my God!"

He was loud enough for the downstairs neighbors to hear and I loved it. I humped myself into the bunched-up covers while Jacob's cries grew wordless and louder still. He yanked my arms, dragging me onto his cock, battering the back of my throat against its stiffness. I sucked hard and let him guide me, no, slam himself into me.

And suddenly he was still, a yell escaping him that was more like a long, hard breath, too intense even for sound. Hot bitterness surged over the back of my tongue and my gag reflex was gone in a haze of pre-scription meds, and I welcomed Jacob's shot, let the come warm me and fill me up. His fingers had gone slack, and I jerked my hands away and grabbed my own cock, fisting it with quick, efficient strokes.

I wanted to just let it rip, but there was the ghost of a dead newborn in the laundry room, and I only had one change of sheets left. At the last moment I clapped my other hand over the tip, and caught my own load as it shot.

I looked up and Jacob was watching with heavy-lidded eyes, and definitely grinning now. I leaned over him to get a tissue from the bedside table and wiped my wet hand with it.

"You should've come on me," he said. I don't know how he can look me in the eye and just say that. Even with the drugs, it wasn't anything I could speak out loud. "You'd look hot, really hot."

I didn't feel like talking about the real reason why I hadn't, so I threw the tissue into the wastebasket and snuggled up beside him instead.

Even though it was three in the morning and Jacob had to be exhausted, he didn't let it go. "Do it next time, okay? I want to see it, shooting all over my chest."

I sighed.

"Okay?"

I rolled over, pulled a pillow against my face and spoke into it. "I have this hangup about the laundry room," I said. Good thing the pillow was there. It sounded even dumber aloud than it had in my head. No wonder I worried about talking dirty; talking in general seemed to escape me.

Jacob pressed himself into my back. His body was much warmer than mine, tacky with sweat, and his chest hair tickled against my shoulder blades. "Okay," he said, and kissed the nape of my neck.

I woke to a slender ray of sunshine streaming through the miniblinds and nailing me directly in the eye. A sharp twinge of pain flared behind my eyeball, somewhere in my brain. "Fuck."

I sat up and looked at the clock. Eight thirty-eight, and my shift started at nine. Not good. I vaulted over Jacob while the pain, apparently fueled by my movement, flared again. I staggered a little as I went into the kitchen and retrieved my cell phone from my jacket pocket. I'd be late, and I was in no shape to drive. I hit memory dial seven, the last programmed number on my phone. Roger Burke.

"Burke here."

I squeezed my eyelids together. Couldn't he just answer with his last name like every other cop? I chalked up my annoyance about the word "here" to my Auracel hangover. "Hi, Roger. It's Vic."

"Oh, hi, Vic!" He was way too happy for a Wednesday. "What's up?"

"Listen, I uh...." I realized I probably should have

rehearsed the way I was going to say it. Damn. And then I remembered his phone message from the day before. "I wanted to take you up on your offer and get a ride from you today."

He didn't miss a beat. "Sure, no problem."

As I searched for a way to end the conversation without explaining any further why I couldn't just drive myself like a regular person, I realized I heard the ambient noise of the Fifth Precinct behind him—the peculiar phone ring and the sound of male laughter as the uniformed cops joked around the water cooler. Christ. Roger was at *work* already and he'd leave to come back and get me? I shook my head. "Gimme, like half an hour," I said, and hung up.

I figured I should at least take a shower so I didn't smell like sex. I washed a couple of aspirin down with a slug of orange juice from the carton and turned the shower on. The room filled with steam. I got under the scalding spray and the pain in my head seemed to lessen a little as my capillaries all opened up.

The shower curtain rustled as Jacob slid in behind me. His chest pressed into my back and he wrapped his arms around my middle. "Morning," he purred.

My cock stirred a little at the feel of a big, hot body behind me, but the pain in my head was more insistent than my groin was. "Hey," I said, and clapped my soapy hands over his to keep them north of the border.

He seemed to pick up on my body language, the way he picks up on everything; he massaged my shoulders, not my cock, as the hot water tumbled over me. "I'm looking at a condo on the lake today," he said. "Why don't you come with me?"

"To make sure it's clean?"

"Clean is good," he said, and his soapy hands slid

down my back, grazed my ass, then slipped back up to work the knots out of my shoulders again. His voice was light and teasing, and I wondered if he was angling to move in together—for real, and not just a temporary, stopgap arrangement.

Jacob nuzzled my wet hair aside and dragged his lips along the back of my neck. My cock started swelling. "Roger's picking me up," I said, and the regret was plain in my voice.

Jacob's lips lingered for a moment, then his hands gave my shoulders a squeeze and he pulled away and reached for the shampoo. "I could've given you a ride," he said.

I felt guilty for not having asked him, but it was just far too gay to have my boyfriend dropping me off at the precinct. "It's your day off." I turned to face him, since it felt too weaselly to lie with my back to him. He seemed fine, concentrating on soaping up his hair.

I rinsed off and slipped out of the shower, and found a week-old towel in the hamper. I left the clean one for Jacob. He climbed out a minute later, water beaded on his olive skin, muscles rippling...with red scratches criss-crossing his thighs.

"What's that?"

He glanced down. "Don't you remember your own handiwork?"

I squinted at the marks. They looked almost as if they'd been made deliberately, like Xs. "Um. No."

He grinned and dried himself off lazily, flexing for me all the while. "Right before you jerked off last night, you got a little rough."

I did? I stared at his thighs. They were just scratches. But still. It really didn't seem like something I'd do, even buzzed. I considered kissing them as some sort of penance, but if I knelt down in front of him on the bathroom floor I'd be asking for a big naked porno scene for Roger to stumble into. I shuddered at the thought.

Which was weird. Roger wasn't bad looking, and a threesome should have been interesting fantasy fodder. I watched Jacob watching me as he dried off. Maybe I was falling in love. I shrugged and finger-combed my hair, dropped my towel on the floor and went to find a clean shirt.

Chapter 3

Roger had stopped at Starbucks on the way to pick me up. He'd even put cream in my coffee. I wanted to be leery of him for being so nice to me, but I chalked it up to his enthusiasm at landing such a prestigious job. Being a PsyCop didn't pay as well as private psychic work, but then there wasn't any call for Stiffs in private work, either. Maybe he was making better money than he had in Buffalo. Or maybe he was a Psych groupie like Jacob. Hard to say until I got to know him a little better.

I looked at him out of the corner of my eye while he drove and tried to get a bead on him, but he was difficult to peg. A regular guy. Probably straight. "So," I said. "Are you, uh, married or anything?" Smooth. Really smooth.

He probably could've put me in my place by responding, "Why, are you? I guess not. The whole station knows you've been shacked up with Detective Marks from the Twelfth since Detective Taylor retired." But, of course, he didn't.

Nope. Roger was the picture of mildly interested surprise. "No, not married. Not seeing anyone." He smiled. "I mean, I just moved here from Buffalo last week."

"Right," I said, wondering how far a straight guy would pursue it.

"You?" he asked.

"Me? Uh, no. Mediums aren't exactly marriage material." Class-five mediums like me, anyway.

"That's a common misperception," Roger said. "In fact, Psychs are just as likely to be married as Non-Psychs, and they have a significantly lower divorce rate."

I considered telling him that the divorce rate was so low because the psychics' spouses probably killed themselves to get away, but I didn't know if he'd appreciate my sense of humor. Not that I even knew if I'd be kidding or not.

Thankfully, I don't live far from the precinct, and we were there before Roger could tell me any more fascinating facts about being psychic.

We reported to Sergeant Warwick's office for the day's assignment. I let Roger lead the way since I was the cause of our lateness. I figured he'd be more difficult to ream out than me, given his cheerful demeanor. Warwick looked up from the files on his desk and motioned for us to sit. No threats, no accusations, no nothing. I made a mental note to use the Roger-goes-first tactic the next time I screwed up.

"Since this is Detective Burke's first day with you in the field," Warwick said, "I'm starting you off with a cold case."

I felt something unclench inside me. Cold cases were a walk on the beach. Maurice and I would grab a box of donuts and take a leisurely drive from scene to scene, me staring out into space and him working on his grocery list. I'd never gotten a hit from a cold case. I'm not really sure why, given the persistence of murder victims. Most likely I was looking in the wrong spots.

Of course, if Lisa had still been my partner, we could've used her precognizant ability to figure out where to focus our energies. Ever since Lisa was a little girl she's played this *sí-no* game, where she could answer any yes or no question correctly. To say the *sí-no* would save us a little legwork would be the understatement of the year. We could figure out which scenes still contained any clues before we'd even left the precinct. Hell, we could figure out if the spirit was even lingering around at all, or if going out to look for it would be an exercise in futility.

But, departmental policies being what they were, Lisa and I would never be partners again. I gathered the files from Warwick and stomped out of his office more sulkily than I'd meant to, but damn it, I thought the policy of pairing a Psych and a Stiff, no matter what the circumstances, was shortsighted and just plain stubborn. The theory is that psychics' energies are complemented by the total sixth-sensory void of a certified Non-Psych, or NP. And while Maurice had been my partner, that had seemed to make a lot of sense.

In retrospect, I think I just got along with Maurice.

I threw myself into the seat at my desk and flipped open the first file. The case involved a child-killer, Terry Lawrence, who'd confessed to a slew of murders and then recanted his confession, saying the police promised him they'd push for an insanity plea if he'd just help them clean house a little by fessing up to a few more missing children. The body of one eight-year-old girl had been found, but five others had never resurfaced. Lawrence's thirty-year sentence was coming up for parole, and the state was hoping that PsyCops could shed some light on the validity of

Lawrence's earlier confessions.

"Where would the spirits be most likely to be found?" Roger asked.

"Where they died, or where they were buried, especially if it was a hide-the-body situation. They get testy when they're not planted right."

Roger took a file from the desk and scanned it. "Since we don't know where they're buried, I'm guessing we need to look at Lawrence's residence."

I shrugged and tried not to let my shitty mood leak out all over Roger. He was a nice enough guy, but he was no Maurice. And he was certainly no Lisa.

Roger seemed unfazed as he did a little typing on his computer. I stared down at another missing child's file and pretended to read. I took a long pull of my coffee. At least the coffee was good.

"Lawrence had a bungalow on Argyle near California."

I pinpointed the area in my mind. "Two blocks from the East River Park."

"That's the place."

If I were Lawrence, I would've dropped the bodies in the river. No doubt the officers working the case had thought of that, even in the seventies. I flipped open the file, and yes, they'd dragged the river as soon as they'd fingered Lawrence as their man. But it'd probably been too late.

I remembered the gape-mouthed face rising up out of the Calumet and shuddered.

Roger's keys were clicking away. He hadn't noticed. "There's a strip mall where the bungalow used to be," he said. "Looks like it's either a gyros place or a cell phone dealer now."

I gulped the rest of my coffee, which had been getting cold anyway, and felt it churn around with my stomach acids. I dropped the cup into the wastebasket. "Let's go and have a look," I sighed.

We pulled up to the cell phone store and found it didn't even open until three. Athens Gyros next door was an uninspired strip mall greasy spoon with a stained acoustic drop ceiling and paneling that dated back to whenever Lawrence's house had been razed. There was a klatch of old ladies nursing diner coffee toward the front of the restaurant, a dark-skinned guy of indeterminate ethnicity reading a paper against one wall, and toward the counter, a mother who looked to be about twelve years old trying to make her squalling kid drink some soda.

"Let's not flash our badges," I told Roger. "Not yet, since we're not investigating anyone here, or even this building. We'll just get…lunch."

It was early enough in the day that the oil in the deep fryer was probably still fresh, so I ordered an extra large curly fry and a couple of Polish sausages. I tacked on a coffee, since I'm a sucker for diner coffee. Roger went with a Greekburger, a side salad and a lemonade. The salad was a little suspicious, but at least he was eating red meat; he probably wasn't some kind of health nut. Did straight guys eat salads? Maurice never had one unless his wife made it. That was about the extent of my knowledge of the eating habits of the heterosexual world.

We slid into an orange plastic booth, me with my coffee and him with his lemonade, and tried to look like something other than cops. I'm usually pretty good at that, since I'm such a slob. And I suppose Roger could've passed for a businessman in his perfectly fitted suit.

Roger stared at me hard as I sipped my coffee, and

not a come-on type of stare, either. God. He expected me to be tuning in my pineal gland even as I waited for my lunch. I wondered how explicitly I'd need to tell him to relax.

I excused myself and went to the bathroom to gather my thoughts and take a piss. The tile was brown, the countertops were orange, and the old light fixtures cast a weird, yellowish illumination on everything. I aimed at the pink urinal cake and peed, focusing on the wall when my piss looked orange in the sickly light. I stared up at some cobwebs in the ceiling corner and thought it would be in my best interest to just lie to Roger and say that it took me a while to attune myself to new situations. PsyCops are like marathon runners. They've got to pace themselves. The rookies have to learn how to take it easy or else they burn out.

Not that he was all that young. I was guessing early thirties. But I was also guessing that he was out to prove something on his first run as a PsyCop. Yeah, lying was the ticket.

Two big Polishes and a steaming platter of fries were waiting for me at the table. Roger hadn't started eating yet, out of some sense of etiquette, I guess. I quelled the urge to roll my eyes. Maurice would've had a hunk of curly fry on his lapel by now.

I sat down and gulped half my coffee, hoping the sixty-something Greek guy who'd taken our order would come around with refills soon. In fact, I was betting on it, since the old ladies looked like they'd been settled into their booth for quite some time and they still had something to sip.

I stuck a fry in my mouth, burnt my tongue, and switched to a Polish instead. It was almost as hot, but there was at least a bun to buffer my tongue. I ate about half of that, leaning over the table so that the mustard and diced onion landed on the tray rather than my sportcoat, and then finished off the rest of my coffee.

I was full already.

Huh.

I hadn't had any breakfast and had hardly touched the fries. Two Polishes with fries should have been about right.

Roger worked on his salad in a quiet, methodical way. I finished my first Polish, then went up to the counter for a glass of water to help me keep the thing down. I almost asked the guy to come around for a refill on my coffee while I was at it, but a rumble in my gut told me to give the coffee a rest.

I walked back to the booth with my red tumbler of water and slid in, my gaze focused inward. "What is it?" Roger asked in a hushed voice. "Do you see anything?"

Oh, that again. I shushed him. "It takes time," I lied.

Roger dutifully clammed up while I figured how many coffees I'd had so far. Two. Okay, the Starbucks was a grande, so maybe it'd counted as a double, or even triple. So the cup at the diner would make four.

Shouldn't have been a problem. I'm a cop. Coffee runs through my veins. I wondered if I could convince Roger to let me run into a grocery store to get some antacids without him tagging along to see what I was buying. I didn't know him well enough to let him see me laid low by a few cups of coffee.

It probably wasn't even the coffee. Maybe it was food poisoning. I tried to remember what I'd had for dinner the night before and came up blank. Lunch, then. I thought back.

Crap, I'd slept through lunch and dinner on an Auracel/Seconal cocktail. And I'd had a donut for breakfast. Could I get food poisoning from a donut? It seemed unlikely, and yet I had felt queasy in the boat.

I glanced up at Roger and he was staring at me like I had the moon landing playing in my eyes. "Anything?" he whispered.

I finally did roll my eyes at his ridiculous persistence—I just couldn't quell it—when I saw a little girl with a pageboy haircut, wearing an atrocious plaid dress. She stood beside Roger, facing me from across the table. The back of the booth practically bisected her from left to right, and her head and shoulders poked out over the top.

I tried to recall if she'd been one of the files I'd scanned earlier, but it was too hard to tell. The photos I'd had were school pictures, kids against garish seventies backgrounds with freakishly fake smiles plastered on and their hair slicked into strange shapes that probably didn't resemble its normal state.

I looked harder at the little girl ghost and there was something off about her. Most ghosts are off in some way, which is why people are scared of them. I looked harder at the girl. Her eyes were too intense, piercing, almost. And her neck looked mottled. When I realized what I was looking at were finger marks, she reached out toward me as if she wanted to hold my hand.

That was different. Usually they talk. I wondered if maybe she'd been a deaf-mute in life.

I hadn't actually expected to feel her touching me, since all the ghosts I'd ever seen were totally noncorporeal. But her fingers were clammy and dead against the back of my hand. A wave of revulsion swept over me and I fought to keep my lunch from coming up. I jerked my arm away, then ran my fingers through my hair in an attempt to cover up the gesture. I had no desire to try talking to her, and even less desire to explain my reasoning to eager Roger. "Let's get out of here," I told Roger calmly. "There's nothing to see."

The kid's ghost followed us but I walked fast, slamming the car door and hoping Roger would get a move on it, too. I pressed my thumb into my forehead but then thought better of it. Some Psychs do that to stimulate their crown chakra; mine was plenty hyper on its own.

Roger fastened his seat belt and started the engine. The little girl ghost stood in the parking spot we'd just backed out of with her thin arms reaching toward the car. "Where to next?" asked Roger. "The park?"

I nodded, while I wondered how I could get him to stop off so that I could get something for my stomach. I racked my brain in an attempt to find something innocuous to purchase, but couldn't think of a single thing I needed. Maybe water. The human body's made up of something like ninety-nine percent water. Water was a perfectly normal thing to need, right?

"Hey," I said as we neared a teeming supermarket. "I need to stop here a second."

I must've sounded casual, since Roger turned on his blinker and pulled into the lot without any questions. "I'll just be in and out," I said, opening my door as he passed by the entrance while his car was still moving, so he'd need to wait for me rather than park and follow. "Need anything?"

He looked a little perplexed at my sudden burst of motion, but he didn't challenge me. "Nope," he said. "I'm good."

Thank God. I jogged through the automatic doors and swerved around a woman who seemed to have twenty or thirty kids in tow. At least six, anyway, and most of them howling. But none of them were trying to put their hands on me, and that was good enough for me.

I trailed along behind them until I felt grounded enough to move on to the drug aisle. I picked up a few rolls of antacids, the small ones that you can hide in your pockets. I remembered a time when I hid more interesting things than antacids in my pockets and I felt sorry for myself. Then I grabbed a water from a refrigerated unit at the end of a checkout line, and rejoined Roger in the car.

"Thirsty," I said, and I toasted him with the water. And then I drank it so I wouldn't have to talk to him while he drove the rest of the way to the park.

I was thankful that the East River looked nothing like the Calumet. It was deep and rushing, and its surface started about twenty feet below street level. Not the type of slow, shallow river in which a guy would bob around in a rowboat.

It occurred to me that if I just hurried up and talked to a dead kid and found out where it was buried, we could go back to the Fifth. Heck, maybe I could even go back home. I turned off my phone so it wouldn't disturb me and started looking in earnest.

We hiked up to the guardrail at the edge of the river and looked down. Someone had drunk a twelve pack of Busch Light and dumped all the cans and even the cardboard box onto the riverbank below. If the river had been higher the litter probably would've floated away by now, but instead it just sat there in the dirt, an unsightly reminder that most people suck.

I bent at the waist and hung over the rail, looking hard for ghosts in the water. But the surface was just grayish, greenish rushing water. Nothing more.

Since a ghost could theoretically hang out on the banks, just like those empty beer cans—great analogy—I hiked up the river, pausing periodically at the guard rail and squinting down into the river. After walking what probably amounted to several city blocks, we came across a black metal footbridge.

I trooped to the center of the bridge with Roger tailing me and stared down, fully expecting to see faces flowing past twenty feet below. Nothing.

We crossed to the other side and combed through that for at least an hour. My stomach continued to churn, and I surreptitiously opened the antacid wrapper inside my pocket with my thumbnail. I crunched on the tablets whenever I could sneak one into my mouth without Roger noticing. I wished I'd eaten something a little blander for lunch, like maybe gruel. It's hard to try to pick out ghosts with your stomach screaming for your attention.

Eventually I spotted a park bench half-hidden among a cluster of scraggly shrubs and made my way over. I sat, and Roger sat beside me. He pulled out a notepad and started writing, presumably detailing all the areas we'd scanned and come up empty.

I cast my mind back to the files from the morning. I'd memorized the kids' first names: Michael, Lucy, Dawn, Hubert... who the hell names their kid Hubert, even in the seventies? Must've been a family name. I pressed my thumb into my forehead. I stared in the direction of the river and actually *tried* to see the kids. Nothing.

I let my breath out and sagged against the park bench, draping my elbows over the back. The cell phone store would be open. I figured we could go back there, scan the place, and call it a day.

I looked at Roger and was about to say as much when I saw it. There was a face in the bush behind Roger's head.

I focused on the face and it grew clear. A man, late thirties-early forties, with the top of his head sliced off.

I wanted to jump back and yell out the first swear word that popped into my head, but there was Roger. I have no idea why, but I just couldn't let Roger know I'd been spooked, just like I wouldn't tell him about my stomachache. Probably it's a guy thing. I just blinked.

The shallowly-decapitated guy's eyes widened, as if he'd just realized that I could see him, or maybe as if he'd just seen me. He'd probably want to tell me what'd happened. Industrial accident. Gruesome mob hit. Whatever.

A hand appeared in the bush beside the face and reached toward me.

"Don't you fucking dare," I snarled, and it was Roger who jumped.

I ignored Roger, went around him, and grabbed at the bush, tearing off a branch. The ghost with the shave-topped head groped at me again.

"What the fuck do you want?" I said, swinging the branch like a baseball bat. It passed right through his hand. "Talk to me, you stupid fuck."

A second head coalesced. It was mutilated like the first, but its scalp flapped from the side of its skull like a bad toupee. Another hand reached out of the bush toward me, and another.

"Stop it," I yelled, swatting the bush with the branch I'd torn off. Another mutilated head appeared, and another. They weren't exact copies of each other, either. Like a bunch of different, unrelated guys got clipped by a ceiling fan on a rampage.

Another pair of hands sprouted out, and another, and something cold and psychically slimy trailed over my wrist where a spectral hand touched me.

I whirled away and ran toward the river, the branch still in my hand. I was screaming, but I didn't give a fuck. I barreled into the guardrail, which clipped me right at hip level, and flung the branch into the rushing water.

"Aaaaaaghhh!"

And then I threw up.

CHAPTER 4

I think if I were anyone else, they would've taken me to the hospital. But...think about it. A guy who sees dead people, and a hospital where people are dropping like flies. Bad combination.

There's a special clinic in the near north suburbs where I fill out inane psychological tests every four months to see if I'm crazy yet and get my prescriptions. It's a low, blond-brick building, constructed ten years ago at the end of a residential street. There's no signage on the building, so I've always just referred to it as "The Clinic." And no one had ever died there. Not yet, anyway.

After my freak-out and apparent collapse, Roger called Warwick, who rushed over in person to take me to The Clinic.

There was a Paranormal Psychiatrist on staff who I'd been seeing so long that he called me "Mister Bayne" instead of "Detective." Dr. Morganstern, man of a thousand sweater vests. He was the one who'd gotten me into the Auracel trials a year before the FDA gave the drug a stamp of approval. I wondered if he had any fun new drugs that would help me hold it together.

A nurse drew a couple vials of blood, took my vitals and ran through my physical symptoms without going into my psychic experience. I've always gotten the impression I was only to discuss those things with Morganstern.

I lay back in a comfy bed, in a room that looked more like a very small hotel suite than a hospital room. The bedspread and curtains were done in a muted floral pattern, and there were a couple of live plants on the dark wood nightstand. I peeked into a cabinet expecting to find a television, but the cabinet was empty. No big deal. If there had actually been a set in there, it probably would've had cable, and so my static station would've been playing all-day soap operas.

There was a brief knock on the door, and a woman in her early thirties who I'd never seen before let herself in. She was slim and pretty, with ash blonde hair cut short and just a little spiky, with glasses so delicate I could've crushed them in the palm of my hand. She wore a boxy sweater over brown corduroys. "Hello," she said, glancing down at a clipboard she carried and then back at me. "I'm Doctor Jennifer Chance."

Oh God. I had a big breakdown in a public park and I had to deal with some doctor I'd never even met? Great, just great. "Is Dr. Morganstern around? Did you page him? Not that there's anything wrong with you—I just want to talk to Dr. Morganstern."

"I'm sorry," Dr. Chance said. I thought I could detect some genuine sympathy there. "Dr. Morganstern is in Japan."

"Oh," I said. And that seemed to be all there was to say about it. I wanted to argue with her, to try to put off doing anything until Morganstern was back, but I wasn't sure my problem, whatever it was, could wait. I didn't realize how attached I was to him until he wasn't there.

Dr. Chance took my account of what had happened

to me, what I'd seen, what I'd done. It seemed odd to me that she wasn't wearing...oh, I dunno. Scrubs. A lab coat. But then again, neither had Dr. Morganstern.

Chance questioned me for nearly an hour, writing notes even as she spoke. I wondered if that was something like being ambidextrous, the ability to speak and write at the same time. I'm lucky I can walk and breathe simultaneously without choking.

Chance shuffled some papers. "Your intake sheet says you vomited and then partially lost consciousness. What have you eaten today?"

"A Polish sausage, a curly fry, some coffee."

"And earlier?"

I felt like a lecture would be coming but there was nothing I could do to avoid it. Then again, I had no reason to think Dr. Chance was the lecturing type. I sighed. "Coffee. And coffee the day before. A donut yesterday morning. That's all."

"Is it common for you to skip meals?"

"No. I don't know. Yeah, I guess." She wrote some notes. "It's a cop thing," I added lamely.

"I'm scheduling an upper G.I. for you first thing in the morning. Eat bland foods as your appetite allows, then no food after midnight, no water after two a.m., and no more coffee today. Got it?"

"You think I have an ulcer, don't you?"

"It's too early to say. But given your medical background, we have to take more precautions than we do with the general public."

Right. It was more likely that the force wanted to keep me alive so they didn't have to go through the trouble of finding and training another Psych.

"Drugs?" she asked.

Shit. I wanted to lie about how much Auracel I'd

taken the day before. I always lied. But they were testing my blood as we spoke, and lying wouldn't get me anywhere.

"Auracel, ninety milligrams about twenty-four hours ago." Chance recorded the number without making me repeat myself, or mentioning that it was triple the highest recommended dosage, or doing a spit-take. I probably should've told her about the Seconal, but Seconal's been discontinued for some time and I didn't exactly get it through a reputable connection. If it showed up in the tests and they called me on it, I could just say I'd forgotten.

"Would you be able to sleep if you stopped your medications until tomorrow morning?"

"Yeah. Of course. I mean, I'm not dependent or anything. I don't take them every day." Just on a bad day. Like a day in which I've seen a bush full of scalped heads.

Just thinking about it made me crave an Auracel with a Seconal chaser.

I made an appointment to return at seven a.m., an ungodly hour, but since I wasn't likely to sleep and couldn't eat, it was probably for the best.

"About the sleeping," I said, wondering if I could get my hands on some barbiturates legally. "If you knew of something that could take the edge off—maybe you could write...."

"We'll see after your blood work comes back. Good night, Detective."

Was it night? I checked the clock on my cell phone. Quarter past seven. I wanted to be home. I wished I'd been born with the ability to teleport instead of hearing the dead. And I wondered if Roger'd bought another cup of coffee for me while he was waiting.

I opened the door to the lobby and nearly bought the idea that my desire to teleport had made it happen; Jacob stared at me from a seat directly across from the door. He had on a pair of jeans, one of his incredibly form-fitting black T-shirts, and a plain leather jacket. He was on his feet and halfway across the room before I even cleared the doorway. "What happened?" he asked me.

I blinked and looked around. A yellow streetlight shone through the thick safety glass on the doorway. The receptionist's window was dark and he was gone for the night. We were alone—except for the surveillance camera that was trained on us. They don't take any chances at modern Psych facilities.

I shook my head. "I dunno. They're doing some tests." I took Jacob by the elbow and steered him toward the door. Despite the fact that there were no faces swarming in the popcorn texture of the walls, no spirits popping out of the philodendrons, I really, really wanted to be home.

Jacob's car was parked in a handicapped spot next to the front door. He opened the passenger door for me and it felt like we were going to the prom. I wondered if anyone was watching. "How'd you end up here?" I asked him. "Did Roger call you?"

Jacob closed my door and got in the driver's side. "Maurice did."

My struggle to figure out how Maurice figured into everything must have shown on my face. "Maurice is your emergency contact," Jacob told me.

"Oh," I said, because that was true. I wondered how Maurice knew to tell Jacob—and then I realized the whole "I'm gay" conversation wasn't going to be necessary at all. "Oh."

CHAPTER 5

"Are you sure you don't want to go to the emergency room?" Jacob asked me for the third time. He was driving with both hands on the wheel and he looked like he'd be happy to run down anyone unlucky enough to get in his way.

"I don't go to hospitals," I said. "I can't. Not without something to block out the ghosts."

Jacob pressed his lips together in a grim line and glared through the windshield.

"This is the same clinic I go to for everything except dental and vision, Jacob. It's fine. It's…it's more than fine. It's the only place qualified to deal with Psychs, and besides that, it's state of the art."

He didn't say anything else for the rest of the ride home, and I was worried he was pissed off at me. I almost apologized to him, except that he was the type of guy who'd probably ask me what I was sorry about, and I wouldn't be able to answer him.

I left Jacob in the kitchen while I flipped on all the lights in the apartment and checked the closet for spectral heads. All clear.

I turned around and found Jacob blocking my way out of the closet. I wondered if he'd appreciate the irony. He stood with his arms crossed, biceps bulging.

It was a pose he'd struck when I'd first met him, in which he'd looked all buff and sexy. Now he looked mostly mad.

"Any idea why Lisa called me from Santa Barbara and told me to leave?"

I eased forward, and Jacob reluctantly allowed me into the bedroom. I sat on the edge of the bed and tried to remember if the message I'd left for Lisa was anything that should've sent her into a tailspin, but I didn't think it had been, even if I had just seen a bunch of submerged heads right before I'd called her.

"No."

Jacob sat down beside me and the bed creaked. He let his breath out slowly. And when he spoke his voice was soft, as if he'd just let all the anger out of himself, too. "I couldn't figure out what she was trying to tell me, and on top of that she was whispering so that I could barely hear. She said you were in danger. From the living and the dead."

Lisa. Did she know how to leave a melodramatic message, or what? Not that I didn't believe her—which is saying a lot, since she was off consorting with the Moonies of her own free will. But until she could give me some specifics, there really wasn't much I could do.

I could feel Jacob staring at me from the side. "That's why I'm worried about that clinic," he said. "What if they don't have your best interests at heart?"

I laughed before I could even control it, an ugly little bark that was too loud and sudden in my stark bedroom. "Christ, Jacob. I'd lay money on it that they don't. The force, the government, whoever...they want a medium. A level five. Can I expect them to keep me comfy and cozy and safe? No. But I can count on them to do what it takes to keep me upright and babbling."

"...and that partner of yours?"

"Roger? You think I need to worry about a guy who buys me Starbucks?"

"Look," said Jacob. "Here's what you should do. Take your cash card, and mine, and withdraw the maximum amount from each account. Then go to the train station and buy a ticket with cash...."

"What? Why should I go anywhere? I don't know what this supposed danger even is. And where would you be in all of this?"

Jacob stared at the side of my cheap white laminated dresser. "Here. Figuring out what's going on."

"You expect me to go somewhere without you?"

Jacob's jaw worked for a moment, and then he put his elbows on his knees and his face in his hands. "You've got to get away from me. Lisa said...."

"Lisa said? You told me you couldn't even understand her!"

"She said I brought it."

I stared. I tried to piece something into that phrase that would make sense of it. What did he bring me? A stomach virus? What about something more insidious...like hope?

I really, really wanted a Seconal.

"Look," I said, doing my best to put on a voice that was incredibly reasonable sounding. I did a pretty good job. "She didn't give you a full message, so we can't act on it. I don't know what she meant. Do you?"

Jacob looked at me sideways.

"That's what's wrong with Psychs," I said. "The sixth sense doesn't match up with the other senses, so anything we describe comes out flawed. It's like trying to describe how purple smells, or what pain sounds like."

Jacob stared at my knee as if he couldn't quite bring

himself to look me in the eye. "But we can't just sit back and do nothing," he said. He'd quieted down, but his voice still held a clipped urgency. "You didn't hear how panicked she sounded."

Good thing. I'd already thrown up and sort of fainted. I didn't need something else to worry about. "It's not going to help for me to go running off," I told Jacob. "If The Clinic, or whoever, is as dangerous as all that, they've probably got some kind of chip in me already."

Jacob finally did look me in the eye, and his face went ashen.

I shrugged. I'd been on a short leash ever since I can remember. That's how I've turned out to be such a liar. "Lisa did her job," I went on, trying to calm Jacob down. "She warned us. Now we know to look out."

"Look out for what?"

I sank back onto my bed and stared up at the ceiling. "Who knows? But if we just play dumb and keep our eyes open, we'll find out."

Jacob made me some eggs and toast and I ate it, and washed it down with orange juice. Breakfast at eleven thirty p.m., since I wasn't supposed to eat after midnight. We curled up on the couch together and watched an old rerun of Ghostbusters. It probably shouldn't have struck me funny, the idea of green, gooey ectoplasm and a bad guy made of marshmallow, but it did.

And the next thing I knew, Jacob was shaking me. And not very gently, either.

"Say something," he said.

"What?" I mumbled, struggling to orient myself. "What?"

"Can you hear me? What day is it? Who's the president?"

"Yes, I don't know, and a horse's ass."

Jacob let go of me. We were on the living room futon with all the lights on and a re-run of Three's Company on TV. Dark showed through a gap in the miniblinds. The VCR blinked 12:00—no help there—but I couldn't have been asleep for long. My heart fluttered in that nervous rhythm it gets when I'm ripped out of the early stages of sleep.

"Were you having a nightmare?" Jacob asked.

If I was, it hadn't been very impressive. I actually didn't have many nightmares. My waking life probably gave my subconscious an inferiority complex. "Uh-uh. Why? Was I talking in my sleep?"

"No. You scratched me."

I gave Jacob a look like I couldn't believe he'd be such a sissy over a scratch, when he turned toward me and I saw the arm of his T-shirt hanging off, a line of bright blood slipping down his arm. "Holy shit! I did that?"

Jacob wadded the remains of his sleeve against his upper biceps. "You're awake now?" He stood cautiously. "I don't want to get blood on your white couch."

"Fuck the couch." I jumped up. "Let me see."

He shook me off and went into the bathroom, where I crowded in behind him. "How bad is it?"

"You're blocking the light," he said. He sounded too calm for someone who was bleeding.

I reached up and flicked on the fluorescent bar over the mirror. It hummed a little, but it was good enough to shave by. "C'mon," I said. "Show me."

Talking to Jacob was like talking to a brick wall. He turned on the cold water tap and then tore his bloody sleeve the rest of the way off. Although he didn't turn so I could see the cut, I got a good look at it in the mirror despite him. It wasn't just one scratch, it was two. They almost looked like a sloppy, upside down "T."

"Shit."

Jacob splashed some water on it and took a look at it in the mirror. It showed up plain for a moment, and then more blood oozed out of it, mixing with the water and running in a rivulet down his arm.

"What did I do that with?" I demanded. I wondered how I could've possibly been asleep while something like that was happening. "Was I sleepwalking?"

Jacob sighed, splashed the cut again, then pulled a big handful of toilet paper off the roll to blot it with. "You weren't sleepwalking. I thought you were...you know...just putting your arms around me in your sleep. And then you scratched me."

"What—with my nails?"

Jacob didn't answer.

He had to be wrong. Not that he'd lie about something like that, but I was sure he'd been mistaken. I must've had something sharp in my hand that I'd dropped while he was shaking me. My fingernails weren't capable of inflicting that kind of damage. I looked down at them with the intention of saying so, and saw they were caked with blood.

I spun out of the bathroom and into the kitchen. I wrenched the kitchen faucet on and thrust my hands beneath it. My vision started tunneling like I was going to have another fucking fainting spell, and I gulped air to keep myself standing. I told myself it was just some congealed blood and not a shred of skin I was pushing out from under my fingernail as I tried to scrub away what I'd done.

I was still washing my hands when Jacob came out of the bathroom. He'd tied a handtowel around the "T" I'd gouged into him.

"Maybe I should go to a motel," he said.

I glanced at the clock. Almost five. "No, don't," I said. "I have to go to the clinic in an hour and a half anyway. I'll stay awake. I'll have some coffee."

Jacob reached over my shoulder and turned off the faucet. He sighed and leaned back against the sink, crossing his arms loosely over his stomach. "It's not me that I'm worried about. It's you."

"Which is why you should stay. We'll watch the early news."

Jacob pinched the bridge of his nose, a weary gesture. He'd been up all night. "Lisa made it sound like I was the problem here, not you. That I needed to get away from you."

"She said that? Specifically?"

Jacob knuckled his eyes, sighed again, and sat down on a kitchen stool. "I don't know what she said specifically, Vic. She took me off guard."

"And then what did you do?"

"I tried to call you," he said, in a "duh" sort of way. "But it went to voicemail."

I looked over at the jacket hanging from my back door. The phone was in the inner pocket and it hadn't made a sound in ages. Cripes. I'd turned it off at the park.

I pulled the phone out of my jacket, flipped it open, and winced. Fifteen phone messages. Lisa, eight times. My own land line: Jacob, I guessed. Maurice, twice. Jacob's cell. Warwick. Maurice again. And Roger.

"Aren't I Mister Popularity?" I said. I hoped I sounded as disgusted as I felt—with myself for leaving my phone off, or with everyone I know waiting until I was at The Clinic to call me, I don't know.

"Did Lisa call?" Jacob asked.

"Yeah."

"Then see if you can make heads or tails of it," he said, and went into the living room.

I wanted to tell Jacob to come back, but there was something so determined about the way he'd walked off that I didn't bother. I looked at my phone in my hand and wondered if it would make a bigger ding in the wall than the coaster had.

But I was the one who'd called Lisa first, back at the river when I'd first seen a cluster of ghostly underwater heads. So I should probably listen to what Lisa had to say.

I accessed my voicemail. "Vic," she whispered. "Shit, I gotta talk to you."

The next message was a hangup. Actually, it was more like a half second of panicked breathing, but I was trying not to think about it. The next four, more of the same. On the seventh message, she finally said something.

"I shouldn't be calling you. I'm not supposed to be talking to anyone. And they told me not to use the *sí-no* on anyone by myself until I take these ethics seminars, but you sounded so bad in your message. Vic, something's really, really wrong. And I can't figure out what it is without knowing what's going on with you. I don't know what to ask...shit."

It cut off abruptly, then picked up again with her next call. "The only person you can trust is Carolyn." There was a second of shaky breathing, some tinny, intercom-sounding announcement whose words I couldn't make out, and a little chime. "I gotta go to the cafeteria or they'll find out I called you. Look, not even Jacob, okay?" She sighed. "Especially Jacob."

I looked at the doorway to the living room. How

could she tell me not to trust Jacob? And how was I supposed to explain that to him? I heard cloth rustling and followed the sound into the bedroom. He was doing exactly what I was afraid he'd be doing: packing a duffel bag. Less than twenty-four hours ago he'd been hinting at getting a place together, and now this.

"She didn't say anything specific," I told him, hoping that I could distract him by talking. "I'm not supposed to trust anybody. That was the gist of it."

He glanced at me and then focused again on tucking a T-shirt into his bag. "She called me up and told me something was wrong and it was because of me. She was pretty pissed off. I tried to get her to go into the *si-no* with me to prove I wasn't doing anything—at least, nothing that I knew of—and she wouldn't even go there. Then she said she was going to get kicked out of the program if they caught her and hung up."

Jacob wasn't going anywhere. That's all there was to it. I stuck my hand into his bag and pulled out the shirt he'd just packed. He stared at it but didn't move to stop me. "Look," I said. "You're here and Lisa isn't, and this *si-no* shit is just too fucking vague. Don't leave."

Jacob fiddled with the duffel bag's strap.

"Please." I took him gently by the chin and turned his face toward mine. When I stared into his eyes, I felt the L-word threatening to come out, but it was too soon, way too soon. I pressed my mouth against his to stop myself from saying anything stupid and he kissed me back, slow but sure. There was a slight hesitation, then Jacob deepened the kiss, his tongue sliding over my lower lip as his fingers abandoned the duffel bag to tangle in my hair.

He got his arm around me and pulled me against him hard, and I had his lower lip between mine, sucking on it, raking it with my teeth, and despite all the horror show it seemed like my life had become, I was hard for him, rocking myself into his hip while his breathing grew rough.

Jacob pulled back from the kiss and looked at me, and his hand tightened in my hair. His eyes looked black, his face flushed and intense. Then he glanced at the clock radio, and I did too. Five thirty. There was enough time before my appointment.

He dragged me down onto the hardwood floor, yanking off my undershirt while I unbuttoned my pants, the same ones I'd worn to work yesterday. Sometime while I'd slept, Jacob had changed into sweatpants and a T-shirt (now missing a sleeve and splattered with a couple drops of blood), and he stripped out of those in no time flat.

We knelt together naked on the floor. My hands moved over the muscles of his chest and belly, brushed against the hardness of his hipbones and clutched him there. I told myself not to scratch him and wondered when exactly I'd turned into Freddy Krueger while I did my best to ignore the towel wrapped around his arm.

Jacob's hands dropped to my ass. He took a cheek in each hand and squeezed, and his fingers pressed into the crack like he could open me right up. My cock must've liked the idea. It stood up straight and poked him in the hip.

Jacob groaned and let go of my ass, swaying back enough to get his hand between us and wrap it around my cock. I gasped, and his mouth covered mine, tongue hot and wet, pressing in.

His hand moved on me, that demanding stroke of his, and my hips flexed in time with his pumping. And then he let go, took me by the hips just like I had him, and eased us apart. "Suck me" he said, his voice low and oh-so-edible, "while I suck you."

I dropped down onto my side and Jacob lowered himself the other way, one hand stroking my thigh while he tucked his other arm under his head. It was a stupid time to have sex, I told myself, what with the disembodied heads and freaky phone calls...and then Jacob's lips slid onto me, just covering my cockhead, and his tongue did a slow tease at my slit.

I pressed my face into his thigh and let out a trembling breath. He sure knew how to make me forget my problems. I dragged my lips downward until my chin settled into the crease of his thigh, then slid my mouth over the musky skin of Jacob's balls. He made a low noise in his throat and took my whole cock into his mouth.

I found the base of Jacob's cock and pressed my lips into it, and felt it swell and harden. I let my breath play over it as I eased my mouth slowly up its length, and ran my tongue carefully over the broad head, and then my own lips, getting everything nice and wet.

Jacob's hand slid around me and grabbed me by the ass again, squeezing me like he really meant business. I wondered if I'd end up in a backless hospital gown at the clinic where the whole staff would get a good look at my white ass with red fingerprints all over it, or maybe even bruises. Jacob nudged my mouth with his cock, and I hoped he did mark me up, fingers, teeth, hickeys, the works. The idea made all my blood surge down to my groin.

I took him by the ass too, squeezed it hard and used it to pull myself against him, stuff his cock as far into my mouth as it would go. Jacob made another inarticulate noise and pulled at my ass again, and then one of his fingers was there, stroking my totally exposed hole.

I pulled my face back a little and then ground it into him hard, clutching at him just as brutally as he grasped me, and the two of us fell into some sort of rhythm, grabbing and squeezing and rocking into each others' faces. I broke first, crying out around his fat cock as he managed to hit all the right nerve endings just at the same time, tongue and lips and fingers all making me crazy. He swallowed like he always did, and his sucking turned from insistent to gentle as he drew my orgasm out, relishing every last twitch he could pull from me.

I got my hand around the base of his cock and started pumping it into my mouth. I felt the cold inrush of air as Jacob gasped around my wet cock, felt his thigh start trembling against my shoulder. It occurred to me that I was going to have stomach tests an hour later, so I pulled off at the first hint of bittersweet, jacked off Jacob's spit-wet cock and felt his hot come splash over my neck.

I settled my head on Jacob's lower thigh and simply lay there with my arm draped over his hips while his breathing evened out. No scratches. No grabby ghost hands. No phone calls. Jacob and I were fine.

Chapter 6

I called the Fifth Precinct on my way to The Clinic and had them list Jacob as my emergency contact along with Maurice. Jacob wanted to come into The Clinic with me, but I made him promise to go to work. He'd only do that after I swore I'd call him to pick me up after the GI series. He gave me a good long look before I got out of the car, and a squeeze on the knee. I forced a smile.

The receptionist's desk was occupied this time, same guy as usual whose name I can never seem to remember. I think of him as, "Nerdy, Horn-Rimmed Glasses," but I doubt he'd appreciate knowing that. I asked him about altering my emergency contact at The Clinic, and he said he'd get the paperwork ready for me while I was having the procedure.

I didn't much care for the word "procedure." I swallowed hard and quelled a Camp Hell flashback. The same nurse from the night before took my pulse and temperature, and instructed me to strip down to my socks, don the pale blue hospital gown and have a seat on the paper-covered exam table. I tried to see if I actually did have Jacob's finger marks on my ass but my neck didn't turn far enough, and there wasn't a mirror in my room.

Moments later, Dr. Chance knocked once and strolled in wearing a very un-doctor like peasant blouse, denim skirt and cork-soled burgundy clogs that I couldn't keep from staring at. She was so focused on her clipboard that the urge welled up in me to flash her my ass and ask if she saw any bruises. And then I assumed that I must be getting panicky if I was fantasizing about doing something that'd probably get me committed. Again.

"How are you feeling this morning, Detective?"

I thought about it, kind of. Actually, it was more like I thought about what to say that would sound normal. "Tired." I said, finally. I figured that'd be reasonable.

Chance kept scanning notes. "Any more alarming sixth-sensory experiences?"

I thought some more. "Uh. Nope."

"Good. And did you have any coffee this morning?"

Oops. I almost had. But then I had this fight with Jacob and we made up in the best possible way. What were we freaked out about again? Lisa? No, something else.

Oh. The scratches.

My stomach churned its own acid. I wondered if I should tell Chance about the scratches. I decided to hold off, since once I said something I wouldn't be able to take it back. Besides, I reasoned. The scratches weren't sixth sensory. They were just fucking weird.

"Detective?"

"No. Nothing since midnight."

Dr. Chance gave me my choice of strawberry or chocolate barium milkshake, with the warning that they tasted like neither. I chose the strawberry. I was then given a club soda-like drink and told to swallow it but not to burp. And then they took a bunch of X-rays.

After I dressed, a nurse offered me a bottle of orange juice and a plastic-wrapped bagel from a vending machine, which I accepted in hopes of flushing the barium out of my system.

By ten o'clock I sat waiting in an exam room for Dr. Chance and her cork-soled clogs. There was a small desk with a chair for the patient beside it. I preferred that chair to the paper-covered table. Chance came in with her clipboard. "We've called the radiologist in and so far your stomach looks normal."

At least some part of me is.

"Your blood work is another story."

I sat very still to keep myself from bashing my head into her desk.

"We're going to have to reconfigure your meds," she said. "Your liver enzymes are high and your liver itself is slightly inflamed."

"Okay." I had no idea what that meant, but I seriously doubted it was anything to mess around with.

"No acetaminophen. If you need a pain reliever, take plain aspirin, and no more than the recommended dose. I see here that you don't drink alcohol. Is that correct?"

"Yes."

"Good. Don't start."

I nodded.

"And no Auracel."

I blinked. "Were you listening when I told you I was seeing heads in the bushes yesterday?" I asked her. I'd also gotten to my feet, somewhere in my panic of having my precious pills taken away. I towered over Chance, who simply looked up at me from the rolling stool at the small Formica desk.

"Regardless of that, Auracel is not an option for you

until your liver enzymes come down."

"And how am I supposed to get my liver enzymes down?" I asked her. Actually, I yelled it.

"We'll take some more blood today and try to determine if you've been exposed to hepatitis, or if this is your liver's reaction to Auracel at such high doses."

"This is bullshit," I said. I'd begun pacing in the narrow aisle between the exam table and a small metal sink on one side, Dr. Chance and my empty chair on the other. "I am a level five medium. You can't just tell me to go cold turkey on the Auracel."

"Detective? Sit down."

I couldn't. I was too pissed off. But I did stop pacing and instead planted my hands on my hips and glared at her.

"I can prescribe a mild sedative in the short term, and remove you from active duty until we determine a course of treatment."

I glared at her some more.

"But right now, all of the FDA-approved anti-psyactives are metabolized by the liver, and we can't risk you taking them until we find out what's going on."

"Even at lower doses?" I asked. And what I meant by that was, the actual dose I was supposed to have been taking all along—one pill twice daily, not three and four at a time.

"Detective," she said, gesturing again toward the chair beside the small desk. I was exhausted, so I gave in and sat.

"You need to be careful specifically because you *are* a level five medium. As such, you are not a candidate for an organ transplant."

I tried to imagine marching around with a dead guy's liver inside of me and my brain nearly leaked out my ears. Dollars to donuts the sonofabitch who'd lost it would be dogging my steps trying to get it back until I was pushing up daisies.

"I want to see Dr. Morganstern," I said.

"He's arranging his return flight, but in the meantime, we're both agreed on this course of action."

I glared at the paper-covered table. Chance kept talking. "And another thing." She slipped a pamphlet into my hands. On the cover was a triangle with a rainbow inside and I nearly spewed the bagel the nurse had given me. Jesus Christ, how'd she know I was gay? It was the blowjob. They'd found traces of semen in my mouth. Oh God, I was so fired. And then I'd lose my health coverage, and then my liver would explode.

"In addition to changing the meds, you'll have to start watching your diet," she said.

I stared at her.

"The USDA modified the food pyramid to reflect their most recent guidelines," she said, as I scrambled to figure out what my diet had to do with being queer. Chance pointed at the pamphlet. "You'll note there's no donut group. And no coffee group either. Limit coffee to one cup a day. Two, at the most."

I looked back down at the pamphlet and read the title. *My Pyramid Plan: a Guide to Healthy Eating.*

Once Dr. Chance and her clogs left, I sat in my backless gown for several minutes staring at the summergreen wall. No anti-psyactives. I could do it. I could. In fact, I was straight most of the week (in the drug sense, anyhow) because it made working easier. And my apartment was clear, as long as I didn't go in the laundry room. And then my liver would stabilize, and everything would be just great.

I ignored the way my hand was shaking when I called Jacob for a ride home.

"Good timing," he said. "We're eating lunch about a mile away at Palatzo. Want me to pick anything up for you?"

I thought of the not-gay brochure I'd stuffed into my back jeans pocket. "Chicken calzone. And a...salad."

"Sure. We're on our way."

Apparently Jacob didn't know me well enough to know I hadn't had a salad in over a year.

But I knew him well enough to figure out that he'd lunched well outside his precinct so he'd be nearby when I called for my ride. Palatzo was okay, but it wasn't worth making a special trip for.

The whole "we" business was a little unsettling, since it meant his partner, Carolyn Brinkman, was with him. Carolyn's only a level two Psych, but she can smell a lie a mile away. At least she paid for her talent by having to be truthful herself, but that price wasn't much consolation for me when I was freaking out about the prospect of life without Auracel. I wished I'd called a cab instead, but it was too late. Jacob had probably already paid for my salad.

I dressed slowly and tried to compose myself. I'd just have to scour my old Camp Hell textbooks and figure out how to deal with unwanted spirit sightings on my own. The books were written before anti-psyactives even existed, so they had to have something I could use. And people ditched ghosts all the time, right? That's what exorcisms were all about.

Okay, maybe not all the time. But it was possible.

I stopped by the receptionist's desk on my way out. Most of it faces the hallway that leads to the exam rooms, but a little window gives access to the waiting room. I noticed the reinforced glass in the little window, like I always did. I wasn't sure if it was to protect the Psychs from the public or the public from the Psychs.

Nerdy Horn-Rimmed Glasses was typing as I tried to slip by, but he snapped-to when my hand touched the doorknob. I don't know why I thought I could get past him anyway; he had to buzz me out.

"Detective Bayne," he said, and I made myself turn toward him. It wasn't his fault I had to reschedule, but who else could I blame? "I have a prescription for you," he said, and suddenly I liked him a whole lot better.

I took the little white bag from him. It felt light. Damn it.

"You're scheduled for fasting blood work for the next five days. Would you like to keep your appointment at seven?"

I ran my hand over my face. Being psychic was such a pain in the ass. "Make it eight," I said. No reason for me to be up with the pigeons if I wasn't on active duty.

The guy clicked around on his computer. "Eight a.m. tomorrow," he said, somehow managing to make it sound incredibly nerdy, and buzzed me out.

I nearly tripped over Roger Burke as I flew out the door. "Oh," I said, since I'd expected Jacob.

"Victor!" He grabbed my hand and shook it vigorously in both of his. He was so happy to see me I almost regretted being off active duty. "How do you feel? Are you okay?"

"Just, um...y'know. Hangin' in there. They took me off active duty for now...tests."

"C'mon." He clapped me on the shoulder in a straight-guy kind of way. At least, I think that was what it was.

I wondered if the Auracel had killed my gaydar along with my liver. "I'll drive you home."

"Um," I said, feeling weird about refusing a ride from someone so eager to please. "That's okay...."

"I picked up some Starbucks on the way here."

Every cell in my body said, "woo-hah." Chance had said I could have one a day, right? And if I had to limit myself to one, it might as well be Starbucks. I wondered how rude it'd be to just take the coffee and decline the ride.

"Well, I've got a friend coming to pick me up," I said. "He's on his way."

"Oh," said Roger, still cheerful, far as I could tell. "Okay." He walked side by side with me to the front door. "But you might as well take the coffee. If you want it, I mean. They'll get cold if I try to drink 'em both myself."

Yay. He offered. "Well, uh, sure. Since you went through the trouble and all. Can I give you anything for it?"

"Nah, it's my 'get well' present." I pulled the door open for Roger as he said this, and he nearly walked smack into Jacob.

Chapter 7

Roger did a little double-take when Jacob didn't step back and apologize like a regular guy might. Jacob stood his ground instead and looked from Roger to me, and raised an eyebrow.

"Oh, hey," I said. "This is Roger, my new partner. Roger, this is Jacob, my, uh...." God, could there be a worse word than "boyfriend?" It made us sound like Barbie and Ken. Or Ken and Ken. Or Ken and G.I. Joe. I told my mind to stop stalling and think of a way to say it. "My partner...at home."

There. I'd said it within the first week of knowing Roger. Now we wouldn't have any awkward conversations looming over us. Or not as awkward as this one, anyway.

Jacob's lips curved into a smile and he held out his hand. "Good to meet you," he said, a teasing lilt to his voice. I had no idea he'd be so tickled about being introduced as my boyfriend. Or whatever.

"Right," Roger said brightly—my guess was that his brightness was covering some discomfort, but that was fine, as long as he wasn't gonna be a dick about it. "Jacob Marks from the Twelfth Precinct. You and your *work* partner are a very well-known PsyCop unit."

Jacob inclined his head graciously. He could take a

compliment like royalty. Then he turned to me. "Ready to go? I think Carolyn's been eyeing your salad."

I didn't particularly care about ditching Roger. I just wanted to get home. "Yeah, okay. Thanks for stopping by to check on me."

"Wait!" Roger dashed to his Crown Vic, a carbon copy of Jacob's, except that it was midnight blue instead of black, and pulled out the Starbucks. "Don't forget your coffee."

"Thanks," I repeated, giving him a salute as I took it. Jacob smirked at me a little as he held the passenger door open for me yet again, but I ignored it.

Carolyn was in the back seat when I climbed into the car. Her tweed suit fit her perfectly, and her blonde hair was swept back into a neat French twist. I couldn't say if she was eyeing my salad, or not.

"I'm not mad," I told her, protecting my coffee as Jacob closed my door for me. We hadn't really talked since a conversation she'd had with Sergeant Warwick resulted in Lisa not only being suspended from duty, but locked up somewhere—"unofficially," of course. Not that Carolyn could've done anything different. She hadn't been able to lie, and Warwick had figured out exactly how to read her silences. She'd been pretty quiet after that.

I peeked over the headrest and she met my eyes. "I know," she said. Good thing I'd actually meant it instead of just saying it to make her feel better. "I just didn't like being the weak link."

Jacob climbed into the driver's seat, shut his door and pulled away from the curb. Roger was still parked, drinking his coffee, and he waved at us as we passed him.

"So that's the guy who's wooing you with coffee," Jacob remarked.

I was about to snap back that I certainly wasn't being wooed when I noticed he was grinning. I calmed down. "Yeah, that's Roger."

Jacob glanced at Carolyn in the rearview. "You'll have to talk to him and ask if he's maneuvering to steal Vic away from me."

"That's really ethical," she said.

I rolled my eyes and concentrated on my coffee. It was good, really good, a bitter, earthy taste that spread through my mouth despite the liberal helping of half & half Roger had added. If I could be bought with coffee, that'd be the right kind.

"I think we should stop by Crash's," Carolyn said, and the smile on Jacob's face died.

"We need to talk about it first," he said.

"We are talking about it—right now. Vic, I have a friend who's an empathic healer. Maybe you'll get better results from him than from Western, pharmaceutical-based medicine. I think you're trying to treat the metaphysical with the physical."

And the physical wasn't even available to me anymore. Not the physical Auracel, at least. I only had a few pills left and my prescription was history, so I'd have to give it up whether I agreed with Dr. Chance or not.

"I dunno," I said. Jacob didn't seem too keen on the faith healer, and I trusted his judgment. "It's kinda physical, too." Jacob looked at me sharply, and I wondered how to avoid talking about what the Auracel was doing to my liver without actually lying, since Carolyn would know. "My meds aren't working out."

"His techniques work on the physical, too," Carolyn said. "It's just a different approach."

Typically I'd scoff at anyone calling themselves a healer. If they had real talent, they would have been scooped up by the pharmaceutical companies, or the government, or some big TV star like Oprah. And if they didn't have real talent, why would I get my hopes up?

But Carolyn was real, and this guy was a friend of hers. And maybe if he could get my liver set right, Chance would let me have my Auracel again. "I guess I'll check it out," I said.

Jacob pulled onto the highway and said nothing, but the way he glared at the car in front of us, I thought laser beams were gonna shoot out of his eyes.

I didn't feel like getting into an argument in front of the Human Polygraph so I concentrated on my coffee. Still good. I sipped and sipped until it was gone, and then I mourned the fact that I had to wait until tomorrow to have any more.

Jacob exited the highway in a neighborhood that had once been Mexican, had then been infiltrated by art school students, and now held an uneasy mixture of poor people and yuppies. We passed a crowded grocery store, a packed arcade, and a tire shop whose entire front was covered in shiny hubcaps.

"There's nowhere to park," Jacob said, and I jumped at the sound of his voice.

We were in front of a Laundromat marked *Lavanderia* when the traffic started to creep. The figure of a Hispanic man coalesced in front of the business, arms crossed over his chest in a defiant stance. He unfurled his arms and reached toward the car, and I could see the outline of the bricks behind him through his arm. Another Hispanic guy with a scraggly mustache appeared beside him, same posture. And another beside him, barely a teenager. And then a big, round Mexican woman with gigantic permed hair. All of their hands grasped at me like they were doing the wave.

"Never anywhere to park," Jacob muttered.

Another group of reaching ghosts waited for us at the intersection. The only time I'd ever seen a group so large was at a blind turn where a whole vanload of tourists had bought it. Jacob's head snapped around as he looked at me, still glaring. "What?"

"Nothing," I said, and then wondered if Carolyn would be morally obliged to pipe in and say that I was lying. Although maybe I was so transparent she didn't need to. "There's a lot of activity around here," I admitted.

"You keep flinching," Jacob said, turning a corner to begin the old no-parking-spot shuffle.

I held myself very still as a guy with half a face ran toward the car, the wreck of his mouth open and his twisted hands extended. Not only had my reality become more *Dawn of the Dead* than I was accustomed to, but suddenly all the hungry cadavers were acting like I was in possession of the world's last brain.

What was with the grabbiness? I was accustomed to ghosts complaining a lot and being insufferably redundant. But the whole touchy-feely thing was fucking creepy.

I knuckled my eyes. "It's kinda bad," I said. I wondered how Carolyn's talents responded to my excessive minimizing.

Jacob rounded another corner with a big mob of ghosts clustered on it and pretty soon we neared the *Lavanderia* again. "I'll drop you off." He pulled over a block down from the *Lavanderia* crowd of specters. "Maybe Crash *can* help you." The laugh lines at the corners of his eyes looked deep, as if the sleepless night he'd had with me was really catching up with him. "Just be careful."

Carolyn and I hopped out during a break in traffic and she steered me onto the sidewalk. Jacob drove away in search of a spot before I could ask him exactly why I needed to be careful. First Lisa, now him. Nonspecific warnings that told me absolutely nothing.

The block we were on had a couple of decrepit storefronts interspersed between a row of sagging three-flats. Latin music floated out of one window and mingled with rap from another. And the storefront we stood before had a cracked plate glass widow dominated by "Tarot - Palm Reader" in flashing blue and pink neon with a big blinking neon hand beneath it.

"You're kidding me," I said.

Carolyn pulled the door open and motioned to a tiny vestibule inside. Its ancient paneling had been painted glossy red and dotted with lavender thumbprints all around. Since there was nobody there, corporeal or otherwise, I went in and headed for the palmist's, telling myself to keep an open mind.

"Not there." Carolyn closed the outer door behind her. "The shop's upstairs."

I looked up the narrow staircase and saw the thumbprints wended their way up. I climbed the creaky stairs with Carolyn right behind me. As we neared the top, I saw a haze of smoke around the single bare bulb. It smelled of burnt sage, incense and cigarettes.

On the second floor landing, the stairs turned and went on to a third floor, but the thumbprints stopped at a frame-and-panel door. The wood was painted yellow with blue stripes, and a sign hung in the center that read "Sticks and Stones" with the words formed out of twigs and semi-precious tumbled gems.

"Here," Carolyn said, but I'd figured that from the

stink of burnt herbs that lingered there. Did the sage keep the ghosts at bay? If so, I wondered if I could manage to use it without burning my apartment building down.

I opened the door into a small shop packed with exotic stuff. A threadbare Oriental carpet covered a hardwood floor that was scratched and dull with age. Racks of scarves and other gypsy-like clothing ran along one wall. Shelves covered with devotional candles—from Saint Agnes to XX Double Cross—covered another. Plexiglas cases full of herbs, trinkets and stones blocked a bead-hung doorway from the rest of the one-room store.

Despite the onslaught of colors, textures, and smells coming from the shop, I turned my focus inward. The little hairs on my arms had stopped standing on end, and my heart was pounding hard more from climbing a flight of stairs than from panicking at the sight of the grasping dead. My panic started to ebb, a little.

Carolyn came in behind me and closed the door. "Crash?" she called.

Latin brass band music drifted up from the street, but a more pleasant *a cappella* number played from somewhere behind that doorway; bluesy and soulful, like a woman with a knockout voice humming to herself while she worked in her kitchen.

The soul music quieted as a hand parted the beaded curtain. A man's hand, wrist covered in black O-ring bracelets and silver on every finger.

"Carolyn!" he cried, and the rest of him (which was equally as decked out as the hand he'd led with) burst through the curtain. Crash was maybe thirty, with spiked-up bleached white hair and a ring through his nose. He wasn't what I'd imagined one of Carolyn's friends would look like. He was hot. Not that I thought anything would happen between the two of us—cheating is the top entry on my "no" list, and I was in a relationship. "I had a premonition that I'd see you today," he said.

"No you didn't," Carolyn said dryly.

Crash clucked his tongue, then looked at me, crossed his tribal-tattooed arms over his chest and raised an eyebrow. "Hey," I said, doing my best to seem like I wasn't in a ghost-panic.

"Hey, yourself."

"This is my friend, Victor," said Carolyn. "We came to see you about healing."

Crash pulled a rough, handmade-looking bowl out from under the counter and placed it on top. It was full of sand. I tried to imagine what he'd use it for: some kind of ritualistic cleansing? And then he lit up a cigarette and flicked the spent match into the sand. "No 'Hi, how are you, I haven't seen you in, what, a month? What've you been up to?' That's so cold."

"I'm sure you're devastated," Carolyn said.

I wondered if all of their friendly banter was this chipper. If so, I hoped I'd never get either of them mad at me.

Crash crooked his finger at me. "I take it you're the volunteer from the audience?"

The humming resumed from beyond the curtain, loud and clear, and although I've never been much for R&B gospel-type music, I really liked it. I stepped forward, just as much to catch more of that music as to let Crash have a look at me.

Crash held up a hand. "That's close enough," he said quietly.

I stopped and wondered if I was so contaminated

that even a guy named "Crash" couldn't deal with my proximity.

"What is it?" Carolyn demanded. "Do you see something?"

"Don't get your panties in a twist, Little Miss PsyCop. I'm not in high gear all the time like you are."

I tried to settle myself. If he thought Carolyn was in high gear, then I was practically in orbit.

"Vic is psychic," Carolyn said.

"Do you mind?" asked Crash. He held his hand palm-out toward her, instead. "I can do it myself."

"I'm just trying to help," Carolyn said, a trace of poutiness in her voice. Crash stared at me, alternating between gnawing at his thumbnail and taking drags off his Camel Light. I stood there like a lump. Carolyn watched Crash watching me.

"He's a medium," she muttered, like she just couldn't keep it in.

"A big overblown TV antenna. Yeah. I get it."

Well. It was the first time anyone'd ever called me *that*.

"Something's unusual about his reception," Carolyn told him. "That's why we came to see you."

"Maybe you should've taken him to Radio Shack." He squinted at me, considering.

"If you're not up to it, just say so," Carolyn said. "It's not like you've got the only metaphysical store in Chicago."

Crash huffed a little and then looked at me. "Only the best one," he said, his eyes boring into mine. "Okay, c'mere."

I shuffled forward another step and he grabbed me by the sleeve of my jean jacket, and dragged me halfway across the Plexiglas countertop. "Hold still," he said. "It's not like I can see the problem written on your forehead."

I was close enough to see his eyes, pale green, like jade. The bluesy humming seemed to intensify as I stared into them. He flashed a tongue stud at me, grazing it across the ridge of his lower teeth. I couldn't tell whether he'd done it on purpose or if it was just a habit.

"You're not right," he said. I thought he'd let go of me with that, tell me to get the hell out of his shop and stop dirtying his vibe.

And then he grinned.

I swallowed. He probably liked it dirty.

He leaned the cigarette into the bowl of sand and slid his fingers down to my bare wrist beneath the sleeve of my jacket. I assumed he'd do something theatrical, but instead he closed his eyes and tilted his head like he was listening to a faint whisper.

Even Carolyn stayed quiet.

Crash let go. "I'd do a gemstone cleanse first," he said. "And once that's done, take a look at fine-tuning."

I snorted before I could even censor myself. Here I was, swarmed with dead and my liver about to explode, and he wanted me to play with crystals? "That's it?"

Crash found his cigarette, took a drag and exhaled slowly so that the smoke drifted around his face. "What did you expect—the numbers for tonight's lottery? You'll have to go downstairs for that. Actually, that's not a bad idea—pretty soon they're gonna replace mediums with radios and video cameras that'll let everyone see spirit energy. The government's got it in the works even as we speak. And then you'll be out of a job."

"Listen," I said. I caught him by the wrist this time, the non-cigarette wrist, and pulled him forward. Not only did he allow it, but he smirked about it like I'd invented some fun new game. "I have a health problem. Can't you tell me something I can use?"

Crash's smirk slipped a little. "I was serious about the gemstone cleanse. If you really are a medium and not just a bullshit artist, it might even help you shield. Unless you live beneath high tension wires, in which case there's nothing to do but move. It's all energy: particles and electrons."

The thought of shielding appealed to me. I'd done it once before—on Jacob, not myself—to keep an incubus from feeling him up. I imagined myself learning to shield so well that I'd be surrounded by an aura so strong and pure that the grasping dead just dissolved on impact.

And then I realized Crash had just called me a fraud. I think.

I suppose I could've flashed my federal license at him and told him I was a fifth level medium, and in fact that was my initial impulse, but I stopped myself before I did. It just felt lame. "How can crystals help me shield?"

I heard the shop's door open and Crash looked over my shoulder instead of answering me. "Well, well, well," he said, and his eyes narrowed.

How could I not turn and look, too? It was Jacob.

Jacob crossed his arms. He was in his suit so he looked reasonably imposing already, but his sleepless night had left him with a don't-fuck-with-me expression that I personally wouldn't have challenged.

"Are you here to tell me you're sorry," said Crash, "or are you just tagging along with Carolyn today?"

Jacob's eyes narrowed. "I'm only the chauffeur."

"How ridiculous, thinking an apology might come out of you, seeing as how you're always right."

I crossed my arms and wished someone had given me a heads-up on the bad blood. I felt vaguely guilty for noticing Crash's looks, but that was stupid. Jacob wouldn't read anything into the wrist-grab. Would he?

"So can you help Victor," asked Jacob, "or is this just another waste of time?"

"I can do plenty," Crash said. He huffed into the back room and left the beads clanking behind him.

I looked at Jacob and he glowered at me as if he dared me to say anything.

I wasn't going there.

Crash knocked the bead curtain aside with a heavy box woven from some kind of cane or bamboo. He slammed it onto the Plexiglas and Carolyn and I winced. Jacob was motionless.

A black woman with a flowered scarf covering her hair followed him out into the main room. She was big, well over two hundred pounds, and looked to be at least sixty. A blue caftan covered her body, hanging loosely over the mounds of her breasts and wide curve of her hips. Her skin was dark and shiny, and she fanned herself with a cheap paper fan printed with the likeness of Saint Anthony. I realized she was the one who'd been humming in the back room. Crash didn't introduce her, and I was too freaked out about the state of my liver and Jacob's big, bad attitude to ask.

Crash pulled a sheet of paper, copied on both sides, out of the basket, and a few baggies of polished stones. He unzipped the baggies and dumped the stones onto the counter, and then considered them. The black woman pointed to a particular stone, and he pulled it out. "I made up this chart that'll tell you how to place the gemstones," he said, working fast as if he just wanted to get our visit over with. "Turquoise, hematite, citrine, rose quartz, sodalite—pay special attention to this one since you're psychic. It'll keep your third eye clean."

He went too fast for me to follow. I hoped the chart was color-coded.

The black woman pointed at a pile that Crash ignored as he scooped everything into a small paper bag. The woman shook her head. "The corresponding colors are on there so it shouldn't be a problem." I tried not to wince outwardly at the thought that maybe he'd read my mind. He began to roll up the bag, and then stopped and looked to the pile the woman had indicated.

She pointed again. "And here," Crash said. "Take this double-terminated smoky quartz, too." He pulled the instructions out of the bag, scribbled something on them, and stuffed them back inside along with the final crystal. The black woman nodded and went back to fanning herself. "Use that one on the brow chakra along with the sodalite."

He thrust the bag into my hands. "That'll be twenty-six fifty."

Chapter 8

The swarms of ghosts seemed thinner when we left Crash's shop, and though none of them came running at me, there were still a lot more of them roaming around than I was accustomed to. Jacob, Carolyn and I walked five blocks to the car in silence.

The ride home was pretty quiet too, until Carolyn spoke with a suddenness that made me jump. "Crash was Jacob's last boyfriend."

Well. The animosity between them made sense. I wasn't jealous, exactly, but the thought of Jacob in bed with someone younger, wilder, and much more self-assured than me didn't do much for my mood. I closed my eyes and sighed.

Jacob didn't say anything.

"They were together for quite a while, six months or so."

"Seven," Jacob muttered.

"That's a long time for Crash."

It's a long time for me, too. Once the truth had been stuffed into the car with us like a big, reeking sack of garbage, Carolyn stopped talking. I wondered how she could deal with so much truth without taking out her service weapon and swallowing a bullet.

We pulled up in front of the apartment and I made a

break for the courtyard gate with my chicken calzone and my bag of rocks. Jacob's quicker than I am, and he was right on my heels. "Carolyn shouldn't have to be the one to tell you what's going on—it should be me. It just never seemed like the right time to go into all of that."

I clutched the bags to my middle and knocked my gate open. The hinges were rusty, and it never rewarded me with a satisfying bang no matter how hard I shoved it. A young black woman materialized to my right, with long blonde hair that was obviously a wig. She wore a pair of short shorts that let her ass cheeks hang out and a lavender tube top. A knife handle protruded from the center of the tube top, right between her breasts, with dark blood seeping out in a big, black circle around it.

"Hey, white boy. You want a date?"

"Jesus," I said, and walked faster. "Go away."

Jacob, who didn't see Jackie, the World's Most Irritating Dead Prostitute, thought I was annoyed with him. Come to think of it, I'd never seen her before, either. I usually just heard her. I tried to look on the bright side; at least now I knew where she was.

The three of us were almost at the vestibule door when I spun around to talk to Jacob. I held my bags out between me and Jackie, and she stared at them, puzzled.

"Jacob, whatever. We've obviously both seen other people. Fine."

He stopped close to me and stared into my eyes. "It doesn't feel fine right now. I'm sorry."

"Don't you be wavin' no bags at me. All I was ax-in' was did you want a little company, and here you go wavin' that shit in my face...."

I turned toward Jackie. I was fairly sure she couldn't

care less about the calzone, but Crash's bag was another story. "That bother you? Huh?"

"Why you be so rude? What I want your skinny white ass for, anyway?" She backed up.

Jacob, meanwhile, had frozen. He was looking in Jackie's general direction, but I doubted he saw her.

I took a step toward Jackie. "What bothers you about it?" I said. "What's it feel like?"

Jackie flung a hand up, palm toward me, dragon-lady fingernails splayed. "You be trippin'," she said, and she backed up some more, the boxy evergreens that bordered the building passing through her thighs. "I ain't gotta take this shit."

And she disappeared.

I looked back at Jacob. "I think this stuff is for real."

He looked at the bag and the furrow between his eyebrows deepened. "I don't doubt it. Crash is for real. I just wish we could've turned to anyone but him."

"Why, what's the matter with him?"

"Nothing's the matter. Just..." he looked over his shoulder at Carolyn in the car. She waited patiently, flipping the radio stations. "Who likes to go crawling back to their ex for a favor after a breakup? It wasn't pretty."

I tried to imagine what anyone I'd dated in the past ten years could possibly do for me and came up empty-handed. "Look," I said. "You get back to work and I'll be here figuring out these stones." And thinking of ways to avoid mentioning my liver. "I'll be fine."

I turned toward my door but Jacob sidestepped and blocked me with his body. He cupped my jaw with one hand, ran his thumb down the side of my cheek, gave me an intense look that I had no idea how to interpret, and then left.

I went upstairs to try and find some way to survive the night without Auracel. Crystals seemed like a pretty lame substitute, but they were all I had. My kitchen counter didn't seem like a sacred enough space to work with them, but I figured it was cleaner than the floor. I upended the bag and let them slide out, then fished around inside for the directions.

What I'd assumed was some kind of fancy computer font turned out to be extremely small, evenly-spaced, cramped handwriting. There was a diagram of a body with the chakras drawn in a row up the spine, starting with the tailbone and ending over the top of the head. That, I remembered from my Camp Hell textbooks. But they had different names than I remembered from my training, and each one had a bunch of other words written around it: wind, metal, water...stuff I'd never associated with chakras.

If that wasn't bad enough, the instructions were clear as mud. "Activate each crystal singly by placing in the receptive hand. Assume *padmasanda*. Avoid clavicular breathing."

Shit.

I left the instructions and rocks on my table and decided to work on my calzone instead. At least I could understand that, even though it was cold and I was too lazy to throw it in the microwave. I tore a chunk out of the middle and threw out the crusts. Then I forced down the salad. It tasted okay, but I wanted to figure out the stupid rocks instead of nibbling on bunny food.

One of my old textbooks was in the living room. Jacob had been reading it and we hadn't gotten around to putting it back in the basement. Or, more accurately, I hadn't been back to my storage closet in the basement since I'd seen the baby's ghost there and so the textbook was gathering dust on my fake mantle.

With the help of the old textbook I made some headway in figuring out how to "activate" the stones. It probably took me ten times longer than it would've if Crash's instructions had been written in plain English.

I muddled through to a point where I was supposed to place the hematite (a.k.a. the black stone) on my crotch and imagine a chakra spinning clockwise. I laid down on the floor, put the hematite in place, and then wondered how to determine clockwise. Was the clock facing me? Or was the clock laying on my crotch for the world to see?

I should probably call Crash. And say what? "Hi, I'm Jacob's new boyfriend, which nobody's told you yet, just to make things as awkward as humanly possible. I'm too retarded to figure out this whole crystal cleanse thing and I'm hoping you'll take pity on me."

Right.

My jean jacket hung over one of my kitchen stools. I glanced at it from my spot on the floor and saw the edge of the white paper pharmacy bag sticking out of its pocket. Still on my back with a rock on my crotch, I reached over and pulled it out. No printed warnings on the bottle like regular people get from real pharmacies. My name, the name of the pill, and the dose. One tablet three times daily with or without food.

I swallowed one of the new pills and thought about taking a nice, long nap, after which everything would all be better.

Sleeping didn't seem to do the trick. It was mid-afternoon when I woke up, and if Jacob was working a case, I probably wouldn't see him until early evening at best.

I sat down in front of the TV and tuned in to Channel

8, figuring that it might help me concentrate on the textbook/cryptic instructions combo. I stared at the static, and let my mind wander. I'd have to talk with Jacob about Crash. I let it go. I should probably tell him about my liver. I let that go, too. It was just me and a speckled blue stone, unactivated, that I thumbed absently while I watched the soothing gray snow swirl on the screen.

And then a face appeared.

I took it for some kind of ghosting from another frequency, like the jazz-hand guy I'd seen the night before. The face's mouth opened and the figure reached toward the camera, and I wondered if it even had been a TV transmission, or a bunch of these dead, grasping fucks in my own living room?

My living room.

My personal space is my sanctuary.

If I didn't have a ghost-free zone to come home to, I'd go nuts. As it was, I could barely stop myself from putting my foot through the little TV. I reminded myself that it might feel good to kick it now, but I'd only have to clean up the broken glass later.

I called Lisa and got her voicemail. Again. I snapped my phone shut and ground my molars together for a while, but that didn't provide any inspiration.

I wanted answers, and Crash was the only person I could think of who might have any. I could have just called him, I guess, but thanks to Lisa, I didn't have much faith in my phone anymore. My meds didn't have any warning about not driving—not that they had any warnings on them at all—so I set off for Crash's neighborhood in person to see which way my clock was supposed to face.

Jackie was sitting on the hood of my car when I went

outside. She filed her nails, pointedly ignoring the bloody shank sticking out of the center of her tube top. She didn't say anything as I got in, but she gave me a nasty look and shook her head as if she'd never seen anything so pathetic. She disappeared when I started the engine.

I took the surface roads to Crash's, not trusting myself on the highway at speeds over thirty miles per hour. The ghosts at the intersections were thick, not just the normal car crashes I was accustomed to, but new ones as well. Little howling kids in hospital gowns with sticklike arms reaching toward me. A screaming couple decked out in full wedding regalia, reaching toward me like they expected me to toss the bouquet. A bunch of moaning guys in uniform with riding boots and bandoleers who grasped at me like a dead army.

They started wandering into the street as I passed. They weren't particularly fast, but they weren't slow like horror movie zombies, either. I swerved around a couple of them but decided it would only get me killed. I started just driving through them, doing my best to make sure that I wasn't plowing into any live pedestrians.

Parking still wasn't fantastic by Crash's store, but I figured it probably never was. It was a neighborhood that'd been built before cars, and had too many people crammed into it today. To claim my spot, I drove though a bag lady with a high-stacked shopping cart. I hesitated at first since she might just be panhandling, then pulled right through her when I saw her arm pass through a lamp post.

A couple of women arguing in Spanish blocked the door to the palmist's shop and I barely stopped myself from trying to walk through them. One of the women flinched as I veered away from her at the last moment, then snapped, "What is your problem?"

I could've pulled my badge on her and given her attitude, but my heart just wasn't in it. I mumbled, "Excuse me," and squeezed into the thumbprint-painted vestibule.

The door closed behind me and something inside me quieted. No more dead. Just me. Crash's building was a safe zone—safer than my own apartment, evidently. I stood there in the vestibule for a second and enjoyed the stillness until I felt more like myself again, and then I took the stairs two at a time and let myself in to Sticks and Stones.

The black woman looked up from the counter and gave me an easy smile.

"Hi," I said. "Is Crash around?"

"He in back," she said, her African American accent thick and kind of soothing, with a little bit of a Southern twang to it. "He playin' on that computer." She shook her head, a little like the way Jackie had shaken hers about me. "He do that all day long."

"Maybe you can help me," I said, thinking that I might not need to deal with Crash at all. I'd expected to be relieved about that, but it felt strangely like disappointment, instead. I swept that idea under the rug for the time being. "I tried to follow these instructions to the letter but I feel like I'm screwing it all up."

I had Crash's diagram in my hand, folded a bunch of times now and a little sweaty from the way I'd been clutching it.

The woman waved it away. "Don't you worry none 'bout that, chil'. It real simple." She pointed to a hematite that Crash had left spilled out on the counter with a bunch of other rocks. "Take that up in your left hand."

I picked it up.

"Now close your eyes, and be still. See the sky, right through the roof of this building. And see the light come down from heaven. That God's love, and it all around you, all the time."

I'm not exactly an atheist, but I can't say I have a clear idea of what "God's love" would look like, if I could actually see it. Still, I dug the idea of something positive and pure around me for a change. I imagined white light surrounding me and the stone.

"All right, now. Hold it. And breathe. And know that God loves you."

I kept my eyes shut for a moment and did my best not to overthink her statement. She probably lived in a world where God loved everyone. Must be nice.

She smiled when I opened my eyes. "It ready now. You put it on your base for protection. Your pants pocket'll do just fine."

I looked at the black stone in my palm. It looked the same, felt the same. But maybe belief was all I needed. "And I just do the same for the rest?" I asked, wondering why there was a need for such an elaborate set of instructions if that was all there was to it. Maybe the word "God" was just too loaded nowadays.

The beads clacked open and Crash flew out of the back room, startling me. "Back for more?" he said.

I looked to the black woman for moral support, but she wandered toward the far end of the counter, fanning herself.

"I, uh...." Something told me that he'd think I was the biggest idiot in the world if I admitted that I couldn't figure out his instructions. "This crystal thing is new to me."

"Carolyn said you were a Psych. I just assumed you'd

gone through the whole certification deal so you could suck off the government's teat."

If that was what I had done, I'd gotten the raw end of the bargain, for sure. "I'm certified, yeah."

"And you can't do a simple crystal cleanse?"

Could he make me feel like even more of an idiot? "They didn't teach that where I trained." Or maybe they did, and I'd been too doped up to notice from huffing spray paint to block out the visions.

He sighed and lit a cigarette. "Okay, fine. I'll go through it with you step by step."

"That's all right." I backed away from the counter and gestured toward the end where I'd last seen the black lady. "Your assistant helped me figure it out."

"Assistant?"

I heaved an inward sigh and wished it were politically correct to say "the great big black woman" without coming off as a jerk. "Your partner?" I tried.

"Partner," he repeated.

"The lady who works here," I said. "I didn't catch her name."

Crash took a long pull off his smoke and crossed his arms. "Don't fuck around."

My mouth worked stupidly in reply.

He glared at me and took another long drag from his cigarette. And then he said, "I'm the only one who works here."

Chapter 9

"Whoever the woman in the flowered scarf is—her. She explained how to activate the stones without all the counterclockwise spinning chakra crap."

Crash blinked at me a few times. "What woman? Where?" he asked, as if he was talking to a small, very stupid child.

I pointed toward the end of the counter. "There. She was working over there." I gestured at a narrow doorway beyond. "She's probably in that room right now."

"That's a closet."

I was starting to get annoyed with him. "Fine, I don't know where she went. The woman who helped you pick out my crystals earlier today."

Crash jabbed his cigarette into the sand and leaned on the counter with both palms flat, eyes narrowed. "Look. I'm not some Stiff you have to wow with the whole psychic routine, got it? I'm a legitimate businessman selling legitimate products. You came to me for help. At least give me the courtesy of dropping this 'Ooh, I'm such a powerful medium' shit."

"What do you mean, shit?"

Crash rolled his eyes and whispered, "I see dead people." He threw his arms wide and his voice went loud. "Come on, man. You get impressions and you know how to read them. So do two to three people out of every hundred if you believe the pabulum that good old Uncle Sam's trying to stuff down your throat. My guess is it's more like seven to ten."

I tried to figure out a defense while Crash ranted at me, but I couldn't quite find one. He wasn't saying I was crazy, and he wasn't exactly saying I was fake, both of which I'd heard too many times to count.

"Look. I do see dead people."

"Okay, you have a perception, I get that. But you've got this terminology that's just designed to feed into the whole 'us and them' mentality that's gonna come back and bite you in the ass the second the right-wing fundamentalists get a chance to burn you at the stake. Instead of 'see' you could call it 'sense,' or 'perceive.'"

"No. I see them."

Crash smirked dismissively and tapped another smoke out of his pack. "Okay, pal. Whatever pays the bills. But don't keep up your act for my benefit. I know how these things work and I don't buy it."

"Christ Almighty," I said, banging my fist on the counter. "Dead people are fucking swarming me and you're trying to tell me I don't see them?"

The black woman appeared again at the end of the counter. I'd been so wrapped up in Crash that I hadn't seen her come in. "No need to be takin' the Lord's name in vain, chil'."

"I'm sorry," I told her. "But he won't listen."

Crash blew smoke in my face. "What—you want me to believe you're seeing ghosts right now?"

I looked at him, and then back at the black woman. She clucked her tongue at my swearing. I wondered why she was so solid and so real it hadn't even occurred to me that she might not be corporeal. And she wasn't grasping at me like the ghosts outside, or telling me over and over how she'd died. "What's your name?" I whispered.

"Miss Mattie," she said, fanning herself. "Short for Matilda."

"Hi. I'm Victor."

"I know," she said, smiling a little sadly. "Be nice to Curtis, all right? He a good boy at heart."

"What's next?" Crash asked me. "Are you gonna tell me I was Cleopatra in a previous life?"

"Who's Curtis?" I asked him.

His eyes narrowed. "So Carolyn told you what my driver's license says. Big fucking deal."

"Oh," I said. I'd stopped yelling back at Crash as soon as Miss Mattie spoke. I guessed she'd had a civilizing influence on me. "Um, who's Miss Mattie, then?"

Crash stared at me, his pale eyebrows knit together in the middle. "Who told you that name?"

"The...um...full-figured African American woman told me. The one in the flowered scarf."

"In my day it was all right to say 'Negro,'" Miss Mattie said. She turned and walked slowly toward the narrow closet door, wide hips swaying beneath her big blue caftan. She disappeared through the door.

My phone vibrated in my pocket.

"What color is her scarf?" Crash asked me.

"I don't know," I said, debating whether or not to take the call. "Lots of colors. She went into your closet and I can't see it anymore."

"So you don't actually *see* her," he said.

I decided I'd better check just in case Dr. Morganstern was back in town. I flipped open the phone and found a text message from Lisa.

"Someone told you about her—who, Carolyn? Jacob?

You're all in this PsyCop bullshit together, aren't you?"

"You could say that," I said absently, scrolling down Lisa's message.

DANGER – YOUNG BLOND MAN NOT WHAT HE SEEMS. SORRY CAN'T TALK.

Shit.

Heart thudding, I turned on my heel and headed toward the door, which was only a few steps away.

"Where are you going?" Crash demanded.

"Police business. Gotta go."

"Oh, shit, you're a cop, too? You don't act like a cop—I thought you were just a consultant or something. Get the hell out here and leave me alone; I've had enough bacon to last me a lifetime. And tell Carolyn I don't want to meet any more of her pig friends."

I briefly considered telling him I was also sleeping with his ex-boyfriend, but decided it might make him mad enough to come after me and deck me. I went back to my car, pretending that the people full of bullet holes and tire tracks weren't swarming all around me, and pulled out my phone. I dialed Lisa's cell.

"Lisa Gutierrez speaking. I won't be available for the next couple of weeks due to my coursework, but leave me a message and I'll get back in touch with you soon."

Damn.

Chapter 10

As I unlocked my front door, I heard someone on TV murmuring in a low, reassuring voice punctuated by sporadic bouts of refined applause. Good thing I hadn't drop-kicked the set. I would've had to explain about it to Jacob.

Then again, if I'd done that, I could've avoided talking about my liver. Or Crash. Or Lisa's weird text message.

The light on my answering machine was solid. "Anyone leave a message while I was out?" I called in the direction of the living room doorway. I opened the fridge to see if food had appeared inside, and lo and behold, it had. The crisper was full of leafy green stuff and there was milk in the milk compartment of the refrigerator door. Also, beer. You know there's a man in my life when there's beer in my fridge, since I can't drink it myself.

Jacob walked to the threshold of the room and stood there framed in the doorway. His black hair was damp, and his olive skin glistened. The gray T-shirt he wore had a vee of sweat at the collar. His expression was neutral, a cop-stare that could mean anything.

"Exercising to PBS?" I asked him. "If someone's gotta do it, I'm glad it's not me."

He broke into a smile that lit up his face. "How are you?" he asked. His tone said, how are you, really?

I shrugged. "Something's up," I said. "I don't know what. But my talent's in overdrive." And I'm not supposed to take Auracel anymore. I didn't say that part out loud, because if Jacob knew why, I could see him enforcing it. I just wasn't in the mood for tough love.

"I saw the stones from Crash in the living room," he said. "Did they help?"

"I dunno. I don't think I did it right." I wondered if I was obligated to tell Jacob I'd just been at Sticks and Stones. If I asked about Miss Mattie, I'd obviously have to get into it.

Jacob had crossed the kitchen and backed me into the refrigerator door before I had a chance to decide whether to talk about my second visit with Crash or not. He seemed to loom over me, broad and hard and radiating heat. Maybe he'd make a move on me and I'd be excused from a conversation I didn't even want to have.

He stopped just in front of me, his body filling my whole field of vision, strangely comforting. I leaned into him for a kiss, but he turned his head just enough to nuzzle his cheek against mine instead. The salty new-sweat scent of him was dizzying up close and I felt my breathing pick up speed.

"I probably should have mentioned Crash before now," he said in my ear, and my rising anticipation flagged.

"Do we have to talk about it right this second?" I asked. I found a vein in his forearm and traced it as it wound around a thick, ropy muscle. I wondered if he'd been bench-pressing the futon.

"I don't want you to think I'm keeping secrets," he said.

"What secrets? I haven't given you a laundry list of the guys I've been with." And then I wondered if he was actually fishing for just that—my history.

"I can count the guys I've been serious about on one hand," I told him. "The last one was Ben and he worked in a record store. We were together four months. Before then...." I cast my mind back through a string of one-night stands and then settled on the boy with the blue hair who'd seemed like he'd be fun. "Mike. He was a hair stylist."

It seemed inadequate to compartmentalize Mike simply by mentioning his job. He'd also had a wicked sense of humor and made a mean omelet. But in the end, I felt like my ghosts brought him down.

"So was Crash," Jacob said. "Before his store. That's how he met Carolyn."

All roads seemed to lead to Crash that night. Did he try to get all of his customers to bleach their hair or was that look reserved especially for him? And did he spin out conspiracy theories while he waxed women's eyebrows? Plant seeds of anarchy while setting permanent waves?

I couldn't picture it.

"Unless you have kids or anything, I really don't need to know," I said.

"He's an empath," Jacob said, veering the conversation yet again towards Crash. "I'm guessing a strong level one. Didn't test high enough for government certification."

I tried to imagine Jacob being with a lover who always knew how he was feeling. Maybe most people possess mundane empathy of a sort, even if it's just an interpretation of their standard five senses. And then I tried to imagine Crash taking a test that could land him an actual job where he might have to take the ring out of his nose and cover up his tattoos with long sleeves, and I didn't doubt that he'd bombed the test. I had no idea what'd possessed him to take it to begin with, since he must've loathed the entire process and everything associated with it.

My own test had been a cinch, at least the medium section. I was high as a kite and the dead guy they brought me to wouldn't shut up. The other parts—clairvoyance, precognition, empathy, telekinesis? Zip. Zilch. Nada.

"I'm gonna work on this crystal cleanse thing." I slipped out from under Jacob's massive gravitational pull. My apartment felt too small, like there wasn't enough space in there for the two of us unless we were having sex.

As a Stiff, Jacob's about as empathic as I am. But he read me well enough anyway. He showered while I set myself up in the bedroom with the diagram and the gemstones, and stayed out of my way for a good couple of hours.

The smell of food brought me out of my cave. I'd cleansed each of the stones and done my best to envision God's love shining on down. It felt stupid, but I figured I didn't have anything to lose by trying.

Jacob had been busy putting my kitchen through paces it'd never seen before. There was a big salad, broiled chicken and even warm bread waiting for me on the countertop. "Wow."

He motioned to one of the tall stools. "I miss my dining room table just now," he said.

"I never had a reason to own one. But look at it this way. You get to sit next to me."

We pulled up to the kitchen counter and ate. I

imagined the world's gayest food pyramid would've been proud of me for getting so many real food groups in.

When we were done, I took the plates and headed for the sink. "I hope you don't mind cleanup detail," Jacob said. His eyelids looked heavy.

"Fair's fair," I said. "You cooked, I'll do the dishes."

He gave me a small smile and headed for the bedroom. By the time I joined him, he was fast asleep, sprawled over most of the bed.

I stripped down to my boxers and reached for the light switch, taking one last look at the man in my bed. He wore only spotless white boxer briefs, and the stretchy material was molded to his impeccable body. The shallow scratches I'd made on his thighs the night before were still visible, though not serious. The T-shaped welt on his upper arm was red and scabbed. I wondered if I should sleep on the futon to make sure I didn't scratch my initials into his chest while we slept. I wondered if maybe he should lock the bedroom door.

That scratching thing had to be some sort of fluke. It probably had something to do with all those needy ghosts I'd been seeing. A stress reaction.

I went back into the kitchen and got another sedative out of my jacket pocket. I'd only taken two so far, and Dr. Chance had said I could take three a day. I wondered if maybe I should take two more; it was nighttime, after all. And maybe the second one would count toward my next day's allotment.

The liver business had me spooked, though, so I took just one, turned off the lights, and squeezed into bed beside Jacob.

As I stared up at the ceiling and waited for the drug to kick in, I considered taking one of my remaining

Seconals along with it, worried some more about my liver, mentally smacked myself for not taking the damn Seconal instead, and then wondered if I could make myself throw the new pill up so I could take a Seconal.

Somewhere in there I guess I fell asleep.

I woke up alone in a darkened room, dead center of my bed with my arms and legs splayed wide. My head was fuzzy and my vision blurred. I forced myself upright while the room tilted around me.

I staggered to the door and threw it open, and was dazzled by the blinding whiteness of the room beyond. Roger's midnight blue Crown Vic was there, with him thrown over the hood. His dress shirt and suitcoat were scrunched up around his ribs and his bare ass showed off its pretty curve where it tilted up to meet Crash's hipbones.

Crash wore a stretched-out old wife-beater with a cracked band logo on the front, and the tribal tattoos covering both arms stood out in stark contrast to his skin. A battered pair of jeans pooled around his ankles.

Crash leered at me like my arrival was just what he'd been waiting for. He grabbed either side of Roger's ass and slammed in hard. "Hey, PsyCop," he said. "How's this for sticking it to the man?"

While I tried to look anywhere but at Roger, the vanishing point of the universe seemed to center on his hazel eyes. "Hi, Victor," he said, and he stretched his far arm out over the hood and held out a Starbucks cup toward me. "Would you like a cup of coffee?"

My knees buckled and there was a roar. My first thought was that I'd been shot. But then I realized I was in my bed, and the room was dark except for the illumination that leaked in from a streetlight outside.

And Jacob was shaking me, hard.

"What?" I said, trying to piece together what was real and what wasn't.

Jacob stopped rattling me, but he held me at arm's length, his fingers digging into the meat of my shoulders.

"What?" I asked him again.

"Are you awake?" Jacob growled.

"I'm awake." I wished I didn't need to know the reason for him waking me, but I supposed there wouldn't be any way out of it.

Jacob let go of me and my shoulders throbbed where he'd grabbed them. We both knelt in the center of the bed, and as he sat back on his heels, I made out a big black "X" through the hair in the center of his chest. I squinted at it and saw a dark trickle ooze down from the corner of the X and spread along the waistband of his immaculate white boxer briefs.

"Holy shit, you're bleeding!" I lunged for the reading lamp on the bedside table and realized I was clutching a cheap plastic ballpoint pen so tightly that my nails had dug into my palm hard enough to break skin.

I stopped and stared at my hand in the dark, unable to grasp the significance of the pen.

Jacob reached past me and turned the light on. The pen tip shone dark red with his blood.

"What the fuck?" I threw the pen in disgust. It picked up no momentum at all and just clattered to the hardwood floor. I glanced wildly at the digital clock. Five after three in the morning. I looked at Jacob, who was poking through his chest hair at the red X I'd gouged into him.

"Were you having a nightmare?" he asked, inscrutably calm.

Images of Crash's tattoos and Roger's earnest face and firm, rounded ass spewed into the forefront of my memory. "Yeah. I mean, no. Just fucked-up dreams."

Jacob grabbed a tissue and blotted his stomach. The tissue turned red.

"I'm sorry," I said stupidly. "I'm so sorry."

He seemed exhausted when he finally stopped smearing the blood around and met my eyes. "How much do you know about the execution I witnessed the other night?"

"What?" I tried perform some sort of check to see if I really was awake this time without doing anything too obvious like pinching myself. "Um, I dunno. Lethal injection, you said."

Jacob held the wet, red glob of tissue to a spot on his ribs where the blood soaked it through. I grabbed another handful of tissues and handed them to him. "Hugo Cooper," he said. "What do you know about him?"

"The murderer?" Given our profession, I would've felt like an ass if I admitted that sometimes the cases start blending together. It wasn't a crime I'd personally worked, it wasn't in my precinct—and it had happened so long ago that I was still trying to figure out how to act like a cop when it was all going down. "He kidnapped three women and he killed them."

"Details," Jacob prompted.

"I dunno. One got away. I guess that means he killed two, right? Or were there four to start with?"

Jacob stared at me hard but I could only shake my head; I had no clue what he was getting at.

"We had a nickname for him down at the Twelfth. I was thinking maybe you'd heard it."

"It was a long time ago." I wished he'd get up and see to the seeping gashes in his middle. "I really don't remember."

Jacob sighed. "It never went to the press. We're care-ful things like that don't leak out, otherwise there'd be melodramatic headlines, copycats, the works. But just among ourselves, we called him the Criss Cross Killer."

I looked at the giant bleeding X on him and my stomach sank.

"Oh."

Jacob stood and made his way toward the bathroom. I sat on the edge of the bed and did my best not to puke.

CHAPTER 11

Jacob and whatever few clothes he kept at my place were out of the apartment by five. He didn't seem mad, exactly, but he had his cop-face on and my nonexistent interpersonal skills were no help in figuring out if he was leaving for now, or leaving for good. He said he was just going to go figure some things out. But how many guys have gone out for a pack of smokes and just kept on going?

Telling Jacob I was sorry didn't do any good. And begging him to stay didn't help. Punching the wall didn't solve anything, either. So I took the handful of stones Crash had sold me and flung them out the living room window.

That felt good for about two seconds, but afterwards I was still me, and my life still sucked.

I wandered from the living room to the kitchen to the bedroom and back about a dozen times, and then it occurred to me that Lisa could help me figure out what was going on. In fact, when you think about it, Lisa owed it to me to help me sort this shit out. It was her half-assed warnings that made Jacob leave.

I called Lisa's cell phone and left her about twenty "call me" messages. Okay, maybe thirty. I texted her. NEED HELP, and CALL ME BACK, and then I couldn't think of anything else to say that I had any chance of typing successfully with my thumb.

I called the operator in Santa Barbara and found there was no listing for PsyTrain, the illustrious program that evidently didn't let its participants have a shred of contact with the outside world. Convinced that they were turning Lisa into the next Patty Hearst, I called the night detective at the Fifth, a tough nicotine-stained broad named Alice who you don't want to rub the wrong way. I talked her into tracking down PsyTrain's phone number with a promise of a case of Diet Coke and a raspberry twist coffee cake.

I called PsyTrain.

Apparently they weren't impressed enough with my credentials to put me through to Lisa. I realized that I probably should have lied and said I was Sergeant Warwick, or maybe even the Police Commissioner, but now it was too late.

I stared at my phone. I put on a pot of coffee and paced through my apartment. In the bedroom, my sheets were rumpled and splattered with Jacob's blood. I wadded them up and stuffed them under the bed. I swallowed a scalding cup of black coffee in one long gulp and then poured myself another cup. Compared to the Starbucks I'd been drinking, it tasted thin and sour, even though I'd brewed it up strong.

I admitted to myself that I had no idea what to do next.

I had to know why I was cutting up Jacob. And I had to know why ghosts were on me like flies on shit. It seemed like Crash might be able to help me, but for every reason I could think of to call him, there was another why I shouldn't. He was legitimate—both Jacob and Carolyn vouched for that. But he never seemed to get a handle on the way my sixth sense actually worked, since it was obviously different from his. And did I really think I could get Jacob back by turning to his ex-lover for yet another favor? Oh, and to top it off, Crash hated me.

There was always Carolyn. She seemed...smart. And blunt. Mostly blunt. It might be good to have the Lie Detector in my corner, but then she'd pipe up whenever I let one loose. Which was probably more often than even I realized.

The only one who could tell me was Lisa. I had to see Lisa.

The idea of driving to Santa Barbara alone was ludicrous—I couldn't read a map to save my life and I'd probably end up in Canada. But finding someone who can drive is a lot easier than figuring out why psychics do the fucked-up things they do.

Maurice. I trusted him enough to help me out. Sure, he'd ask questions. You don't just drive someone across the country without asking questions. I paced back and forth in front of my bay window, and the glaring overhead light bounced my reflection back at me through the slats of my miniblinds as I tried to figure out how to approach him. I'd have to tell him that I was playing tic-tac-toe on Jacob in my sleep. He'd already figured out Jacob and I were together, but I'd have to come right out and say it. Awkward. But who else could I turn to?

My cell phone buzzed and I nearly tripped over a Camp Hell textbook trying to get to it. It was Lisa, it had to be. She knew how badly I needed to talk to her. She'd tell me what to do.

I flipped open the phone and my heart sank. It was Roger. "Hey," he said. "I hope I'm not bothering you.

But I was out jogging and I saw your lights on. Are you up for Starbucks?"

I nudged the blinds aside and looked out past the courtyard. A reversed image of my living room over-laid the gray pre-dawn street below, but if I shifted my focus, I could pick out details. Traffic was sparse but regular, commuters who needed to be downtown by seven. Roger stood on the far sidewalk in sweats and a T-shirt, waving.

Roger—stupid Roger. I didn't want Roger, I wanted Lisa. And yet, there Roger was, always willing to lend a hand. Or give me a ride.

I wondered if Roger was so eager to please that he'd take his midnight blue Crown Vic on a little spin to California. Then I wouldn't have to burden Maurice with the gruesome details of my sex life.

"Coffee sounds great," I said. "I'll be down in five."

Roger did his best not to look surprised when I asked him to drive me to California. He suggested flying, but commercial airlines were out of the question. All it would take was one airplane-bound ghost to turn me into an air-rage psycho.

"Driving it is." He toasted me with his espresso. "I'll need half an hour to get my things together. Bring a suit. We'll want to look official when we get to the PsyTrain facility."

I had a jacket that didn't look like it'd been slept in, I thought.

"And your prescriptions—have you got a couple of weeks' worth?"

"I dunno. I'll just have to make whatever I've got last. I'm not going back to The Clinic and announcing that

I'm going out of town. I'll just have to call them and reschedule my fasting bloodwork. I don't want them involved. Warwick, either."

"Warwick's easy. You're on medical leave. Just check in with him on your cell phone and act like you're still in town."

Hooray for the cell phone. If Maurice was looking for me, he'd try that number, too. I could just tell him I was on a lot of meds and he wouldn't ask any questions. If Jacob was looking for me....

I didn't know if Jacob would be looking for me or running as fast as he could in the opposite direction. He'd told me he just needed to get some rest so he could think clearly. I had no idea what that was supposed to mean.

Roger and I were packed up and on the road by noon. He went over the route to Santa Barbara with me and I glazed over somewhere in Oklahoma. I hadn't taken one of my new pills since the night before. I figured I'd better save them in case things got ugly in the motel and I needed to knock myself out.

City traffic was spotty, as city traffic tends to be, but in another hour we'd hit the highway, passed through the suburbs and were driving through cornfields and skirting small, rural towns and the occasional strip mall. Rural Illinois: corn country.

"I don't want to pry," Roger said, reaching to turn down the top-forty station that played more ads than music, "but why didn't you ask Detective Marks to go to PsyTrain with you? He's a lot more intimidating than I am. And if they're being stubborn about letting you see Detective Gutierrez...."

Miss Mattie was more intimidating than Roger was. But I doubted he was fishing for a validation of his manliness. He wanted to know what was up with me and Jacob. "He'd probably want to go through the proper channels," I said. "And I don't have the time."

"Really?" We passed a field dotted with cows. "I heard he wasn't above bending the rules. Take that case with the shapeshifter where you used Detective Gutierrez' abilities even after you were specifically told not to."

Shit. He'd done his homework. No big surprise. "I dunno. I guess I just don't want to get him any more tangled up in this."

"In what, Vic? What are we doing?"

I sighed. We'd been on the road for a couple of hours. He could turn the Crown Vic back around and be rid of me easily enough. Heck, he could pull over and dump me by the side of the road, too. "Something's up," I said. "You know how my talent's been a little...overly sensitive lately?"

"Yeah?"

"There's something else, too. It's gonna sound a little crazy..." like anything having to do with PsyCops sounded rational. "But it's almost like I'm contaminated. There was this murderer who was executed a few nights ago, and it's like I'm acting out his M.O. in my sleep."

"You're channeling?"

My third cup of coffee lurched in my stomach at the thought of a spirit using my body like a wetsuit. "I dunno. I've never done any channeling. Not on purpose, anyway. I think you need really solid defenses to mess around with that shit."

"And you don't have them? Solid defenses, I mean?"

I pressed my tacky forehead against the passenger window. "I thought I did. I mean, the dead used to just stick to the places where they died—if not that, then their graves, or some other place that meant a lot to them. But now it's like they're coming out of the woodwork and following me."

Roger drove in silence for a while. I fished around in my pocket for a sedative. The thought of all those cold, pale, grasping hands was making me antsy.

"What do they do? When they follow you."

I had a pill on my tongue, so I swallowed before I answered him. "I...I dunno. They grab at me."

"Have you tried talking to them? Asking them what they want?"

"Look, Roger, the dead aren't rational people," I said. Maybe he was just playing Devil's advocate, but I felt my adrenaline surging as if I needed to protect myself. "You can't just have a conversation with them. It's not like they're gonna give me a message and then be satisfied and go away—that's Hollywood bullshit. They don't have a message and they don't have a purpose and they don't go anywhere."

"So when there's an earthbound spirit, it's around forever?"

"Jesus, I don't know. There aren't enough mediums around to help the researchers come up with a solid theory. And it's too fucking subjective."

Roger glanced at me. He looked concerned, in a mild and boyish way. "But what do you think, Vic? You've had this ability your whole life. You must've put some kind of logic to it."

Actually, I'd had it since I was twelve. Close enough. "I guess they disappear over time," I said. "Otherwise I'd be fighting my way through mobs of Neanderthal spirits."

"Makes sense."

"Sometimes I think that ghosts are people who were

unhappy in life," I said. It wasn't very scientific or very accurate, but it was an idea I've always had in the back of my head. I'd never really voiced it, since I couldn't help but think of what it would mean for me once my time was up.

Chapter 12

We hit a big snarl of traffic in Saint Louis around six in the evening. We stopped to pick up some burgers, but I ended up getting swarmed by dead in the drive-through line and making Roger hit the road again before he had a chance to order.

The spirits thinned out once we were on the highway again. I offered to take the wheel for a while, if Roger could keep me on our route, but he told me there really wasn't anywhere to pull over.

I took another pill since Roger didn't need me to drive, and soon we'd gone past all the suburbs and made our way through more farmland again. I stared out at the stubbly, shorn fields dotted with gargantuan rolls of hay, glad that we were in an area that wasn't particularly populated since I'd had my share of ghosts for the day. A transparent hitchhiker with hollow eyes appeared just as I thought that. He reached out toward me as the Crown Vic sped past him.

It'd been dark a couple of hours by the time Roger pulled up to a B&B somewhere in the middle of rural nowhere. I would've preferred a Super 8, a newer construction that had less potential for ghost activity, but every time we passed by a likely motel, Roger waved it away and said he was still good to drive.

"I dunno about this place," I told Roger. "An old farmhouse, probably full of dead...farmers."

"Just take a look," he said. "We'll ask to see the rooms before we commit to anything."

Nobody swarmed me as I got out of the car; a good sign. We knocked on the front door and stood shivering on the porch for a good ten minutes before a burly guy with a gray crew cut came to let us in. He said that a double-occupancy room was available, if we wanted it. It felt funny to think of sharing a room with Roger, but since we'd just spent the past ten hours together in a much smaller space, I told myself there was nothing weird about it.

The room was kind of goofy and overdone, with hunter green wainscoting and wallpaper with a fishing motif. At least it wasn't all hearts and flowers; it would've been way too weird to wake up next to Roger in a room that looked like a honeymoon suite, especially since I'd had that dream about him and Crash.

There weren't any spirits lingering around, and that's what mattered the most. Roger booked the room while I got our overnight bags out of the car.

There was a television tucked into a bureau at the foot of the two double beds, but I hadn't been interested in TV since I realized I was getting reception from the other side in my own living room. An ancient rotary phone sat on the table between the beds, black plastic with a fat, curly cord connecting the handset to the phone. I wondered if it even worked. Maybe, maybe not. But it gave me an idea. "Do you need anything?" Roger asked me, reaching for the remote.

I needed lots of things, but I figured Roger was already doing everything he possibly could for me.

"I'm fine." I wished the new pills were as strong as

Seconal. Dr. Chance had said they were sedatives, but they didn't seem to be relaxing me at all. I pulled the plain bottle out of my pocket and looked at it, and wondered if it was just some kind of placebo. Lisa would be able to tell me if they were real or not without a shadow of a doubt.

I went into the bathroom, ran the water to cover the sound of my voice, and flipped open my phone. Years of acting secretive had stuck with me, and even though Roger and I were neck deep in the whole California plan, I still only wanted him to know only as much as I absolutely had to tell him. The reception bars on the phone's screen were tall, which was a relief since we were miles from civilization as I knew it. My thumb was poised to hit the memory dial to Lisa's cell when the phone vibrated in my hand, startling me. I dropped it and it made a huge sound against the hunter green tile floor.

"Everything okay?" Roger called.

I gnawed at the inside of my cheek and quelled the impulse to tell him I was still "fucking fine," since I could hardly get testy with him given everything he'd done for me. Still, the mother hen routine was starting to get old, and fast.

"Dropped my toothbrush," I said, wishing I could've thought of something heavier on the spur of the moment. "Unlisted" showed on the screen, and I debated letting it go to voicemail. It could be Warwick checking up on me. It could be Jacob, who I was dying to talk to—and yet if he knew what I was doing he'd probably try to talk me out of it. And it could be Lisa.

I picked up. "Bayne," I said, keeping my voice low.

"This is Victor, the medium, right?" A man's voice, definitely not Lisa.

"Yes."

"Okay, yeah. I was just wondering about Miss Mattie."

Recognition clicked in. It was Crash. He'd probably gotten my number from Miss Can't-Tell-a-Lie.

"Now is really not a good time."

"I acted like a dick before, you know? But it just blew my mind when you said you were talking to Miss Mattie."

The mirror started fogging up. I turned the cold tap higher. "I'm right in the middle of...."

"I've been thinking about her all day. She was our next-door neighbor—died when I was just a kid. But she always said I had the 'gift.' Like she did."

Shit. I wanted Crash to go away. I wanted to talk to Lisa. "Uh huh."

"So is she, like, watching me all the time?"

I sighed and drew a big happy face on the fogged up mirror with my fingertip, then smudged it out with my palm. "No. She comes and goes."

"That's a relief. 'Cos I know a few moves that'd probably kill her all over again if she saw 'em."

I did my best not to imagine him naked.

"I can show you some, if you wanna come over."

I closed my eyes and wished he hadn't just said that. "I don't think so."

"C'mon, man. I know you want to." He said "know" in such a way that I was sure he'd picked it up from me while we were grabbing wrists.

I sighed. "I'm in a relationship right now," I said. I wasn't sure whether or not that was actually true, since Jacob had left. A huge pang of loss swept over me, and I perched on the edge of the clawfoot tub so the emptiness didn't bowl me over.

"No one has to know," he said, a smile in his voice.

"With Jacob," I added, because maybe if I insisted that it was the case, he'd come back.

At least the statement was enough to take the wind out of Crash's sails. "Well, well, well. Didn't take Jacob very long to find himself a shiny new psychic to show him some parlor tricks, did it?"

I had no idea. I just wanted to talk to Lisa.

"I'd invite you both over, but he's kind of a prude about three-ways. And besides, he's pissed off at me."

"Looked like it went both ways," I said.

"I never told him I was a saint. He just expected me to act like one and got all high-and-mighty when I didn't."

Good to know about the cheating. It just confirmed what I already believed: that it's pretty low to polish your rod on the side, and Jacob wouldn't have any of it. Sure, I was busy racing across the country with another guy, in an attempt to get a straight answer out of Lisa as to why I was turning Jacob into mincemeat. But it was still good to know.

Maybe Crash had called for a reason—other than the fact that he wanted to get in my pants. Maybe Miss Mattie was guiding his hand. Or fate.

"Listen," I said, glad for a reason to change the subject. "Is there any way to shield if you haven't got any crystals or stuff like that?"

Crash snorted. "Like what, the 'white balloon' trick they teach in KinderPsych?"

I closed my eyes and wished I hadn't even asked. I might have been better off not knowing my training was about as advanced as a five-year-old's. I really, really wanted to talk to Lisa. "Okay, then. I gotta go."

"Whatever. The invitation still stands. With Jacob or without."

He hung up and left me staring dry-mouthed at the

ugly tile floor.

Roger knocked softly. "You okay in there? Do you see something?"

I stood and looked at the mirror, half expecting to find a ghoulish apparition reaching for my reflection, but I was alone. Odd, considering the age of the building, but after all I'd been through, I wasn't going to complain. "Nope," I called. "All clear." I tried Lisa's cell phone again and got the same damn message I'd gotten since she'd settled in at PsyTrain. I texted CALL ME yet again. And then I splashed some water on my face so I looked like I'd been doing something other than hiding with my phone in the bathroom.

Roger lay back in one bed with ESPN playing on the TV when I emerged, a cloud of steam trailing behind me.

"You sure you're okay? You don't look so good."

I ran my fingers through my hair. "I think it's this new medication," I said. "It's supposed to calm me down, but I'm totally wired." I'd also had six more cups of coffee than I was supposed to that day. Not that I was counting.

"What is it?" he asked. "Is it an anti-psyactive?"

"Just a sedative."

"I've got some muscle relaxants for a shoulder spasm I had a couple of months ago. They're not very strong, but maybe they'd take the edge off?"

I was about to decline, but Roger was already up and rifling through his bag. It couldn't hurt to try, I figured. Muscle relaxants didn't seem to amp up the ghosts like alcohol did, and maybe a mild dose really would help me get some rest.

Roger set the bottle on the table between the two beds. I lay down on my bed, picked it up and read it.

The pharmacy's address was in Buffalo. One-half to one tablet as needed, up to four per day. That seemed like a pretty broad range. How strong could they be?

I opened up the bottle and tapped a round orange pill onto my palm. There was a line down the middle where it could be broken in half. I considered taking half, briefly. Then I swallowed a whole pill. I've never been the kind of person to do things halfway.

Roger handed me a bottle of water from a tiny refrigerator beside his bed. I took a swallow and lay back on my pillow and stared at the ceiling. I didn't feel anything. But it'd be too soon. And it probably wouldn't be all that dramatic, anyhow. Just a little something to help me sleep.

The ESPN sportscasters droned on over the squeak of sneakers on a basketball court, and I wondered where they were broadcasting basketball from in October. Was it basketball season in China? Did they even play basketball in China? The sportscasters didn't sound Chinese. I considered opening my eyes to see who was playing but it felt like way too much effort. I drifted off to the sound of rubber soles on hardwood.

CHAPTER 13

My dreams were vivid, floaty, and downright pleasant. I was drinking coffee in a coffee shop full of hot young men. Crash was behind the counter with his spiked blond hair, giving me a knowing come-hither look every time he caught my eye, and flashing the tongue stud to make sure I knew that if I consented to spend a little naked time with him, I wouldn't be sorry. Some of the murder victims from my last case were there, too: the guy with the Scotty dog collection was yukking it up with the buff architect. At a table in the far corner, the goth boy who'd broken my heart in the mid-eighties was licking the foam from a latte off his black-painted lips in a way that sent a major rush straight to my groin.

But best of all, Jacob was there, right across the table from me—shirtless and unscratched. His perfectly sculpted arms and chest gleamed like he'd just come from a bodybuilding competition, and his eyes, which had seemed so pinched with fatigue and concern lately, were just deep and melty and oh-so-sexy. Jacob reached under the table and ran his fingers up my thigh. I don't normally go in for public displays of affection, but since we were in the world's gayest coffee house, and everyone else there seemed to have sex on the brain too, I let myself relax into Jacob's caress.

Something buzzed against my thigh and I did a double-take at Jacob. A vibrator? In public? My cock stiffened and I slouched lower. I was shocked that he'd do something so dirty where anyone could see, but it turned me on nonetheless.

The vibrator pulsed against my leg, and I caught my lower lip between my teeth. I'm not a big sex-toy aficionado, but damn, it was sexy. And Crash was right over there with that tongue stud...maybe Jacob wasn't as uptight as Crash had thought. Maybe he just needed to be approached the right way....

The buzzing drilled into my thigh.

"Higher," I told Jacob.

The buzz pulsed again.

I woke up to the feel of my phone going off in my pocket. My head was wooly and my tongue was, too. I looked around the room. A single reading lamp was on, and Roger's bed was rumpled. Roger was gone. My phone vibrated again.

I flipped it open. Lisa. "Hello?" I said, and the word came out a little slurred.

"Vic? Oh my God, Vic, where are you?"

I looked around at the trout wallpaper. "In the fishing room."

"You sound funny—are you okay?"

I found the idea of her asking me a yes or no question pretty amusing. "I dunno," I said. "Am I?"

"You're on drugs? Yes. Okay, what kind? Wait, never mind, it doesn't matter. Are you alone? Yes."

"If you say so."

"You're not safe. You need to get out of there."

I looked up at a bad oil painting of a couple of guys casting their lines from an old, scenic bridge and wondered if it was going to fall off the wall and decapitate me. "Why?"

"I don't know," she said. "Ask me some questions so I can figure it out."

"You warned me about Crash." I stared down at the tent of my hard-on pressing up against my jeans. "What was I in danger of there—a killer orgasm?"

Lisa sighed. "I have no idea what you're talking about, Victor, and you're all messed up. What's Crash? Some kind of drug?"

"Maybe," I said, sitting up. My head spun a little and I paused to enjoy the feeling. "Or maybe he's a young blond man."

"No."

"Yes he is."

"No. He's not the one."

The clipped, hushed tone of her voice was a buzzkill, but it got me to thinking. I knew another blond man who was younger than me. "Is it Roger?"

"Yes!"

"It can't be. Roger's helping me get to California so I can talk to you."

"No he isn't. Victor, listen to me. Wherever you are, just get up and go. Is he nearby? Yes."

PsyTrain had taught Lisa how to ask her own questions. Useful, but something she probably could've figured out without flying across the damn country and going incommunicado. I stood up and the room dipped a little, but I had pretty good sea legs from years of chemical experimentation. I went to the door and turned the handle. Locked. I took a look at the lock. It was shiny and new. And very sturdy. "I'm locked in. Lemme find my gun."

My shoulder holster was draped over a desk chair

beneath my jean jacket. It was empty. "Did Roger take my gun?"

"Yes."

I closed my eyes and wished the room would stop spinning. "Was that a muscle relaxant he gave me?"

"Yes."

"Was it as mild as he said it was?"

"No."

There was some background noise on Lisa's end. I heard her cover the phone and say, "Not now, this is really important. Who? Oh my God, really?" She got back on the phone with me. "Vic, Jacob's here."

I was busy staring at my empty holster. "Where, in California? How'd he get there? Are you shitting me?"

She'd stopped listening to me, though. "Yeah, I'm on the phone with him right now. I don't think he knows where he is."

"Vic." Jacob had taken Lisa's phone away from her. "Something's going on. We're going to get to the bottom of it."

A key turned in the lock, and I decided there wasn't any more time for me to play twenty questions. "Someone's coming, gotta go." I flipped off my phone, stuck it in my pocket and fell back into bed, feigning sleep. I forced myself to take slow, even breaths, and I even let my eyes flicker back and forth a little bit under my lids.

The door to the fishing room opened. "Vic?" Roger called softly. "Are you awake?"

I moved my eyes around under my closed lids and said nothing. The orderlies at Camp Hell usually fell for the fake R.E.M. routine. And after a long, horrible pause, it seemed like Roger did, too.

I heard him move quietly around the room, stopping

for a moment at the television armoire, and then at my jean jacket. Fabric rustled, and then the floorboards creaked softly as he approached the bed. I wished I could see through my eyelids. I wondered if some psychics actually could; heck, I've heard of weirder talents. Why not see-through eyelids?

I probably would've flinched when he put his hand on me if not for the muscle relaxant. The pill had delayed my reaction time long enough to give me some kind of doped-up control over myself. I wondered if I was still sporting wood from my dirty dream, if he was gonna cop a feel while I was out cold. It didn't seem like a Roger kind of thing to do, but when it was all said and done, how well did I know Roger, anyway?

He made a little "tch" noise in his throat, whatever that meant, his hand slipped into my pocket, and he took my phone. Damn. I felt like a wuss for not trying to fight him off, springing into action and taking him by surprise, but he had both his gun and mine, and I was doped-up and slow.

He stayed there in the room and eventually I must've drifted off again, thanks to the pills. I have no idea how long it was before the sound of a key in the lock woke me. I lay still with my eyes shut and listened.

"How long has he been out?" Though it was a whisper, the female voice seemed vaguely familiar.

"Most of the night."

Fabric rustled and something was set down and unzipped. "We could probably wake him up," whispered the woman. "Or we can wait until it's light out. We don't want to blow it after we've gotten this far."

Roger sighed and moved to his own bed. It creaked gently as he settled on it. "We've waited this long. What's another couple of hours?"

I personally wished they'd just wake me up and get on with whatever they had in mind. Since they thought I was asleep, I had to just lay there and wonder what the fuck was going on. I had no idea if I normally shifted and rolled around in my sleep, and if so, how much. So I had to be perfectly still for what seemed like forever to the sound of quiet footsteps, the gentle rustle of paper and the occasional sigh.

Eventually I couldn't take the not knowing anymore and I rolled onto my side and opened my eyes. Roger was there, propped in his bed, watching me intently. "Hey, Vic," he said. "How're you feeling?"

Like I could kill someone, except someone had taken my gun. "I dunno," I lied. "Okay."

"Detective Bayne?" said the female voice, and I turned and found Dr. Chance standing at the foot of my bed. She wasn't wearing the hippie-chick ensemble she'd had on at the clinic—instead she wore a black knit suit, casual but smart, cut to just cover something at her waist that looked suspiciously like a gun belt. I wondered if maybe she was a Fed.

"Dr. Chance?" I did my best to sound bewildered. I was actually a little surprised to see her, but I tried to make it look like I hadn't realized anyone was there besides me and Roger.

"That's right," she said. "Do you mind if I take your vitals?"

I sat up. "Why? Am I sick?"

She pulled a stethoscope and blood pressure cuff out of a bag. She handled them confidently enough that I assumed she actually was a doctor—but what if she wasn't? If only I'd been born with the *si-no* instead of a direct line to the afterlife, I'd know.

"Just checking to make sure you haven't had an

adverse reaction to the new meds."

"No, they're fine," I said as she velcroed the cuff onto my biceps. "But they don't work anywhere near as well as the Auracel."

She nodded and stuck a digital thermometer in my mouth, pumped up the cuff so tightly it hurt, then let some air out in a slow hiss. "That's to be expected. They function differently than your old medication."

She shone a penlight into each of my eyes. "Everything's normal," she told me, and I swallowed back a laugh. "Now, listen. You might feel a little light-headed, but what I have to tell you is very important: we've got access to some new medication that will alter your ability to communicate with the dead. If you work with us, I think we can get your hypersensitivity under control."

That part of the plan sounded fine, until she opened a small case that contained a dozen pre-filled syringes. My heart pounded. It's not a fear of needles or anything. It's just more Camp Hell baggage. "What's that?"

"The latest in anti-psyactives." She swabbed the crook of my arm with an antiseptic wipe, flicked the syringe a couple of times, then looked at me over the rim of her glasses. "You do want to get your visions under control, don't you?"

"I think half an Auracel would do the trick. Maybe we could adjust my dose...."

Roger stood behind her with his hand resting on his holstered gun. He didn't look like his normal cheerful self, and I doubted he was going to offer to go get me some Starbucks.

"Detective," said Chance. "This is the cutting edge of current Psy research. You're lucky to be a part of it."

Oh God. Cutting edge. Just like Camp Hell, back in

the day. My breathing went shallow and rapid and I tensed up to spring.

"Hold him," Chance said, her voice bland.

Roger was airborne in less than a second. His forearm snapped my jaw shut and wedged under my chin; his hard, muscled body pinned mine; his upper thigh drove into my groin, and he forced my arm out to the side with its white, vulnerable, undersurface extended. I struggled to move—knee-jerk reaction, I guess, since I'd still be drugged and locked in a room even if I managed to throw Roger. Not that my stunted flailing even budged him.

"Just a pinprick," Chance said. There was a sting on my inner elbow and then warmth spread through my arm.

My panic died away immediately and I went limp. A rush of well-being stole over me and I had to admit that Chance's new miracle drug wasn't half bad.

"That's better," said Chance, and Roger climbed off me. "To get a baseline, I'm going to need to ask you some questions."

She started firing them off, grilling me about the type of contact I had with the dead, the frequency and intensity, and my ability to pull information from them that they might not want to part with.

I answered her as best I could, but the overwhelming feeling of good cheer coursing through my veins was far more interesting to me than Chance. Would I get access to this wonderdrug if I helped them test it out? Would it eventually be available in some kind of syrup or pill so I didn't have to poke holes in my arm?

"Let's move on to your level of control," she said. "If you tell a spirit to do something, does it generally comply?"

"I dunno. No, not really. They're kinda stupid, can't usually tell you much other than the way they died." My headrush ebbed a little, and it occurred to me that I felt an awful lot like I did when I was celebrating with a fresh batch of Seconal.

Chance looked at her watch. "How's the medication? Shall we try a supporting dose?"

I don't think it was actually a question. I wasn't sure how much time had gone by, but not long, maybe ten minutes since Roger had bodyslammed me. He held me again—just my arm this time—and she shot a little more juice into me. There was the warmth, and the wonderful, wonderful high.

"Try to recall a time when you successfully encouraged a dead subject to talk about something other than its own passing."

"A guy in a coffee shop...I used him as a witness." I laughed. "Don't tell anyone, it's off the record."

"And so you would say that you might possess the ability to command dead subjects, maybe with more training?"

I pressed the back of my head into the headboard and rode the wave of contentment that had taken hold of me. It felt so much like Seconal that it made me wonder if it was laced with barbiturates. Yeah, that made sense. Barbiturates were a drug group that I could understand.

"Detective?"

"Depends on the dead."

"How so?"

"I think this guy wanted to talk to me because he just liked to talk. Probably was the sort of guy who never shut up when he was alive."

A word popped into my head: Amytal. Seconal's

close cousin. Also known as truth serum. Not that it actually makes anyone tell the truth; confessions taken with the aid of Amytal aren't admissible in court. But it keeps the subject in happy, la-la, everybody's-my-friend land. I'd have to concede that I was currently visiting that very spot.

"Detective Bayne?"

"Huh?"

"Your assessment of the amount of personality retained by the deceased?"

I thought about it. "I've always thought that they're more like the living when they're fresh."

Chance nodded. "It might have to do with the degradation of their signal over time."

"Signal?"

There was a rap on the door. Roger left his post at my bedside and opened it. The guy with the crew cut who'd let us in the night before stuck his head inside. "There's a deputy here," he said quietly. "I'll try not to let him upstairs, but there's only so much I can do. If I tell him to go get a search warrant, he'll get suspicious."

"I'll handle it," said Roger.

"He thinks I've got a honeymooning couple here. He wanted to see both of you."

Chance looked at me. "How're you doing on that medication, Detective?"

"Fine," I said. My voice sounded a little distant.

She pulled out another syringe and shot it into me without even bothering to ask Roger to hold me down. I closed my eyes and enjoyed the headrush.

"He'll be sedated for at least fifteen minutes. Longer, if he falls asleep," she said. "Let's go." They left the room and locked the door behind them.

I sat up. Did they really think I was out for the count?

I felt loose-limbed and high, sure. But my years of self-medicating with Seconal must've built up some kind of tolerance. And here I'd thought the quality of the pills had been going down.

Chapter 14

The jarring sound of an old-fashioned phone ringing startled me out of my dazed inertia. I stared at the gigantic plastic behemoth on the table between the beds. It rang again. I picked it up and held it to my ear. It might be Chance calling from downstairs, after all, acting like everything between us was hunky-dory and she was really concerned about my well being.

"Vic?"

Except if it was Chance, she was doing a pretty damn good impression of Jacob.

"How did you get this number?" I whispered, worried that Chance and Roger had heard it ring and were making tracks back to the room. Frankly, I was shocked that they'd take my cell and leave a working phone just sitting there beside me. But since I was in a hotel, maybe outgoing calls were blocked. Incoming calls were apparently free game.

"Lisa narrowed it down. You're in Missouri, twenty miles away from a town of any size. The sheriff sent someone over, but I really couldn't give him much to go on."

"Crap." I steadied myself against the headboard and tried to remain upright. "I'm locked in a room and they've got my cell phone and my gun. What do I do?"

"I'm putting you on speakerphone," said Jacob. "Okay. Ask us something Lisa can work with."

I racked my brain for a question other than, "What can I do?" Yes or no, I told myself. "The door's locked," I said. "Is there anything in here I can open it with?"

"No."

"Can I get out through the window?"

"No."

I pushed the curtain aside. A decorative metal grating covered the outside of the window. In the country, on the second floor? Why?

"If I make lots of noise, will the deputy hear me?"

"No."

"They didn't pick this place out at random," I said, "Did they?"

"No."

"Who else is there besides Roger?" Jacob asked.

"The guy who let us in—it seems like he's in on it. And Dr. Chance," I said, "if that's even her name. If she even is a doctor."

"He's in on it," said Lisa. "And Chance is a doctor."

"Think," Jacob said. "Is there anything you can use as a weapon?"

"Against two armed people?" I tried to keep an edge of hysteria out of my voice. "Should I just keep going along with them?"

Lisa huffed in frustration. "Too complicated. I can't tell."

"There must be something I can do," I said.

"Yes."

"Jesus fucking Christ, what?"

"You're not helping," she said. "Yes or no questions."

A bark of a laugh worked its way through. "Is it bigger than a breadbox?"

"Yes."

I looked all around the room. "The desk?"

"No."

"One of the beds?"

"No."

"The TV?"

"Yes," Lisa said cautiously. "Yes and no. Look at it and tell me what...."

I heard a key turning in the lock and cut her off. "They're back," I said, and hung up the phone. I threw myself into bed and tried to look medicated.

The door swung open and Crewcut Guy peeked his head in to check on me. I lay there with my eyelids nearly shut and didn't move. He stared at me for a while, then closed and locked the door again.

I stared at the rotary dial for a long moment and then my stomach sank. I'd planned on doing a star-69 to get Lisa back on the phone, but there was no star. I picked up the handset. There was no dial tone, either. My theory about the outgoing calls must have been on the mark.

I looked back at the big wooden bureau that housed the TV. That had to be it—though what "it" was, exactly, I hadn't figured out. I opened the door and looked at the set. Nothing unusual there. I tried the drawers. Empty. There was maybe an inch of clearance between the bureau and the wall. I peeked behind it and saw a mess of cables.

It seemed like a lot of cables for a TV hookup. Maybe they had satellite. That would explain the off-season basketball game. I searched for the remote but came up empty-handed. That didn't make any sense. I could see Roger taking my gun and my cell phone. But the remote?

I swung around and started pulling and pushing at the TV set, hoping to find something, anything I could use, before Roger and Chance got back.

Something clicked on the front of the television set as I yanked on it, and the big tube tilted forward into my hands. I had no idea what the inside of a television was supposed to look like, but I suspected that the panel of hidden knobs and LCD readouts weren't standard-issue. A slim DVD player was duct-taped to the inside. I figured that probably explained the basketball game.

I could just take a handful of wires and yank them out—but what would that possibly accomplish? I wished Lisa would call me back and tell me what to do. Unplug the thing? Smash it? Change the settings?

I forced myself to think. If Roger and Chance wanted me dead, I'd be dead. They needed me alive, presumably for my talent. I saw myself hooked up to a gurney, electrodes wired to my head and a bunch of IVs feeding into my arm, and my vision started to tunnel. Camp Hell all over again.

Damn it. It wasn't the time to be crying over Camp Hell, not now.

Okay. So there was a machine and it was doing something electrical. It was on. I could turn it up or down.

I turned some dials up. The numbers on the LCDs increased, but nothing happened, at least that I could tell. I turned them down.

A big black guy in a turn-of-the-century butler's uniform appeared beside me. He reached for me and I backed away.

A thin girl with Mary Pickford hair in a floor-length nightgown appeared to my right. She reached toward me too.

"Don't touch me," I snapped, but it didn't look like she heard. I began to back off from both of them but decided I should probably peek over my shoulder first to make sure I wasn't headed for anything creepier.

Dr. Morganstern stood behind me. "Holy shit," I cried. How did he get to Missouri? Had he ever really been in Japan? "You're in on it too?"

He pointed at the TV guts. "Turn the second dial up a little," he said. "You'll filter out the older ones."

The little girl was trying to grab my arm, but the farther I got from her, the farther I'd be from the TV. The room was small enough that she'd grab me eventually, and if not her, the black guy would. I grabbed the second knob and turned it the opposite way, and she seemed to dissolve. The butler grew very faint.

"Not so much," said a faraway voice. I turned around and Dr. Morganstern was almost as transparent as the butler.

"You're dead?"

He pointed at the console, and I turned the knob down just a little. Morganstern grew more substantial. But so did the butler, who got his hand around my wrist.

I felt resistance, and then a little give as his hand slipped inside my forearm. "Holy fucking God," I yelped, and pulled my arm away. "Don't you dare get in me."

"Try the other dials," said Morganstern.

"Which one?" I demanded, wondering if wrapping myself in tin foil would help, since supposedly everything was made of particles and electrons. Not that I had any tin foil.

I twisted another knob and the butler got really solid.

I imagined a white bubble around him—my very lame method of shielding, on par with hopscotch and pixy stix. The ghost seemed puzzled by it for a fraction of a second, but it was enough for me to spin down the second knob before he used me for a human condom. He grew faint.

I turned back to Morganstern. He was solid enough. "My God," I said. "You stuck around just to help me?"

"Not exactly." He looked somewhat abashed. "I'm following Roger Burke. But that's all I can seem to do with him. Follow."

I shook my head, trying to wrap my head around the idea that someone I knew—and knew pretty well—had died. "Isn't there some kind of light you're supposed to go toward?"

"You were wrong, back there in the car. Sometimes people do have one more message, one more task to complete, before they can move on."

"But why...?"

"Put it back together." Morganstern pointed at the TV. "They're coming."

"Shit." I snapped the TV up and closed the bureau, then flopped down on the bed. If Chance took my pulse again, I'd be fucked. My heart was pounding double-time.

"Detective," Chance said as she came through the door, Roger hot on her heels. "How are those meds doing?"

"Fine," I said. "I'm fine. I think I'm good for now."

"They want you to go along with them," said Morganstern, "but they're terrified that you won't. They were just going to pay you off at first, but Roger got a look at that bank balance you never touch and decided that money wasn't a viable incentive."

Roger'd been stealing my mail. Great, just great. I did my best to relax and look out-of-it. If I could pull off a decent fake stupor, I'd have plenty of time to be pissed off later, once I gave them the slip.

Chance pulled up a chair. There was no discussion of moving me, so I figured they'd gotten rid of the deputy easily enough. "Let's talk about the increase in spirit activity you've been experiencing."

"Okay."

"It's those pills she gave you," said Morganstern. "They're psyactives, and they're opening your power up so that it runs both ways. You've been shining like a beacon to the dead." He pointed a ghostly finger at Roger. "This one's been slipping them into your coffee until Chance found an opportunity to just give you the pills and trick you into taking them. And they fed you that line about your liver so you wouldn't counteract the drug with your Auracel."

My liver was okay? The Hallelujah Chorus started to play in my head.

"We'd like to do some tests with you," said Chance, talking at the same time as Morganstern. "See if it's possible for you to command the spirits once they're in visual range."

"They want to get you to use spirits to blackmail people," said Morganstern. "They'll tell you it's to fine-tune that new drug, or that electronic technology. But once you're part of their inner circle, they'll want more funding. Lots of it."

"I hate tests," I groaned.

The lock tumbled and the guy with the crewcut came back into the room. "That deputy's back, and now he's got three more with him. We should abort."

Chance looked hard at me. "Out of the question."

She brushed my hair back from my forehead in an eerily tender fashion.

"Go along with her," said Morganstern, "or Burke will murder you. Like he did me."

Oh. So that was why he was following Roger. Morganstern had never struck me as a particularly vengeful man, but then again, I only knew him as my doctor. Not the dead husband of a widowed woman, or the dead father who wouldn't walk his daughter down the aisle. Dead people are pretty big on grudges.

Chance's hand lingered at my temple. "Detective Bayne is perfect for our project. You want to be part of this groundbreaking Psy research," she said to me, "don't you?"

Morganstern seemed to know what he was talking about, and I struggled to figure out how to play along without seeming as if aliens had landed and turned me into a pod person. I gave Chance a vacant grin, and did my best to look like an oblivious, doped-up fool. "You're the one with the meds."

The tension left the room as if I'd found the magical switch. I couldn't be bribed with money, since no amount of money ever brought me peace. But it was entirely plausible that I could be bought with drugs. Morganstern smiled and nodded; I must've been convincing.

Chance smiled, too. "I'm going to have Roger drive you to another safehouse while I talk to the deputies. I'll do everything I can to keep you comfortable, Detective. You and I have got a lot of work to do together."

Chance left with Crewcut Guy while Roger turned to gather our bags.

"Do something," said Morganstern.

I did a palms-up gesture at him. What was I supposed

to do? The Amytal had started to wear off, but come on. I was no match for Roger, especially unarmed.

"Mister Bayne, you've got to get him while you're alone."

Roger shrugged his blazer on, and stuffed my jacket in a bag. He disappeared into the bathroom. "He'd kick my ass," I whispered. "What do you expect me to do?"

Morganstern looked down at the remaining syringes by the side of the bed. "Amytal. Inject it into an artery and you'll subdue him immediately."

"That's easy for you to say. Sure—I'll just find an artery. And I'll ask him real nice to hold still while I do it."

Roger came back into the main room with a damp washcloth, and started wiping our prints off all the surfaces.

"It's the only way," said Morganstern.

I gave him my best "yeah, right" look.

"If you can't do it, then let me."

I swallowed hard and slid a syringe into my pocket while Roger's back was turned. I'd relied on Morganstern in life, but I wasn't sure he was entirely trustworthy in death. What if he didn't want to leave me once he got under my skin? Would he march around inside my body forever, leaving my friends to wonder when I'd taken to wearing sweater vests?

And what if a shot of Amytal to the artery would kill Roger? Without Carolyn or Lisa to back me up, I had no way of knowing if Morganstern was using me for revenge.

Roger threw the washcloth into the bathroom, snapped up the case of syringes and drew his gun. "C'mon, Bayne. Time to go."

I stood and the room dipped—I guess I was still

woozier than I'd thought. Morganstern hovered beside me, and said, "You've got to subdue him. It's the only way."

Roger got a shoulder under my armpit to help me to the door, and I fumbled between us to try and palm the syringe in my pocket. My hand brushed against his hip, and he stopped hauling me along and cringed back. "Touch me again and I'll blow your hand off, faggot." He resumed hustling me toward the door.

It wasn't the threat that did it; it was the realization that Roger would just as soon shoot me as not, regardless of how integral I was to their precious operation. Because I was queer.

"Okay," I whispered. Roger would think I was talking to him, but it was really aimed at Morganstern. I did my best to relax.

I felt Morganstern entering, like the sickening rush of an unfamiliar drug. He came through somewhere in my core and extended himself into my extremities, arms and legs, fingers and toes. I felt numb and disconnected as Morganstern settled in. And then my body surged into action.

My hand whipped the syringe out and flicked the protective cap off with my thumb, holding it as easily as I might have held a pencil, or a gun. I stuck the needle into Roger's neck and plunged in one smooth motion. Roger raised his gun and started to pull the trigger—and then collapsed with his double-action semi-automatic just another small squeeze from putting a hole in my forehead.

I made to reach for Roger's gun but I couldn't move. "Get the gun," I tried to say, and I guess Morganstern understood. I picked up the semi-automatic and felt myself jerked toward the door before I could even see if Roger was still breathing. My body jogged to the end of the hall and down a back staircase I hadn't known about, heading unerringly toward a way out.

Morganstern stopped me at the back door, twisted the knob a few times, and then tried harder.

"It's locked," I thought. "The more you rattle it, the worse you're making things."

The room lurched and I was myself again, with a semi-transparent Morganstern standing beside me. "Can't you kick the door in?" he demanded. "Or shoot the lock out?"

"You watch too many cop shows," I told him, noting that my mouth worked again. I raised a hand, and that worked, too. I pulled the curtains aside on the back hall window. It was barred.

I would have to shoot the lock out, after all—though I doubted it would be as neat or efficient as they make it out to be in the movies. I tore down a curtain and wrapped my arm and hand to give it some kind of protection from the spray of wood and metal I was about to cause, took aim at the lock at the best angle I could figure, and squeezed.

The gun popped and there was a clatter of metal. There were also shouts and running footsteps. "Drop the gun and put your hands above your head," someone shouted.

I didn't think it was Crewcut Guy, but I didn't know for sure. I spun around and found a pair of men in sheriff's khakis pounding down the hallway toward me, weapons drawn. I started to put my gun up, but then I hesitated. What if Chance had an inside man there, too? They'd infiltrated my precinct and my clinic—why not the sheriff's department where they'd planted the safe house?

"Drop the gun," the deputy barked, as the hall behind him filled with more bodies.

Someone farther back in the mob that'd crowded into the building called out, "That's all right—that's my partner."

Maurice pushed his way to the front and my hand fell to my side, heavy. The deputies stood down. Maurice smiled and held a hand out to me. "C'mon, Victor," he said. "Let's get out of here."

CHAPTER 15

The Lawrence County Sheriff's Department seemed like a decent enough group of guys. I'm not sure if any of them were psychic. If so, it was probably a low-level talent who'd never been certified, but was sensitive enough to notice that something just wasn't right about the B&B, or the guy with the crewcut, or maybe Jennifer Chance as the blushing bride. Crewcut Guy would've taken me down at the rear stairway if a couple of deputies hadn't already had him trussed up in the back of their SUV.

Even though these fine, corn-fed deputies had just saved my ass, I let Maurice handle the problem of getting me alone in the vicinity of Roger Burke to get a statement from Morganstern. Statements from dead people aren't considered hard evidence, but they go a long way in turning up the paydirt.

Maurice had this way of telling people what to do without being bossy, and then making them feel good for doing it. He managed to explain that I was a level five medium without creeping them out, and got them to agree to let me talk to Morganstern while Maurice gave his own statement.

The initial rush of Amytal had worn off, but I still felt woozy and off my game. I sat in a storage closet that abutted the holding cell where they'd dumped Roger Burke, and I used a mini cassette recorder that Maurice kept in his glove box for those times when I was too wrecked to write. Good thing he hadn't cleaned out his glovebox since he'd retired.

"They've been planning this for almost a year," Morganstern said. "Once they got the technology to this point, they targeted some mediums and put together these safe houses."

Hearsay. Morganstern had only been dead about ten days and didn't know about their planning process firsthand. But still, I repeated his statement into the recorder. It might turn out to be useful later.

"Why'd they take me across state lines?" I asked him. "Won't that bring in the Feds?" Something inside me withered a little at the prospect of dealing with the Feds again, like I hadn't seen enough of them after the incubus serial killer. I wondered if I'd need to get an apartment in Missouri so that I could finish all the damn paperwork.

"It's six of one, half-dozen of the other," said Morganstern. "Ideally, they could just recruit you and then nobody would come after them. But if things went sour, either the Feds would figure them out or the Chicago Police Department would. They figured the locals had more to lose by your disappearing and could move a heck of a lot faster, so they took you out of local jurisdiction. There were safehouses in Wisconsin, Indiana and Iowa, too. They were just looking for a way to lure you into one."

I wondered if I would've noticed Roger driving me north to Wisconsin on our trip to California and blanched. Probably not. I'd be too busy looking for ghosts. And then I wondered if every safehouse had one of those nifty GhosTVs. I conveniently paraphrased Morganstern's last statement to say, "They had several safehouses in adjoining states," without mentioning specifics. I wanted one of those TVs.

I'd scored some cold medicine on the way to the Sheriff's Department. It was a sloppy way to counteract whatever traces of psyactives were left in my system, but it was the best I could do without a prescription and a pharmacy in a major metropolitan area. The ghosts weren't reaching for me anymore and trying to slip inside. But I would've given my left nut for an Auracel.

My statement to Sheriff Wilkes was kind of a blur. Since the only thing I needed to keep to myself was the location of the other three safehouses, I let everything else just spill out. I got the impression—not that my people-skills are anything to write home about—that Wilkes found the whole thing pretty farfetched, but that he was doing his best to be professional and cover all the bases.

Wilkes was an older guy, maybe sixty-five, pushing seventy, with a thick head of steel-gray hair and serious bulldog jowls. He looked like he'd never cracked a smile in his life. He asked me a few preliminaries and then just let me get my story out, disjointed and patchy as it was. I told him about Roger. I told him about Chance. I told him about the B&B and Crewcut Guy and the Amytal and the TV. Wilkes didn't make me repeat anything—you know, the way you do to imply that someone's bullshitting—so my whole schpiel took maybe an hour. I probably could have gone on a little longer, but my tongue was sandy, my concentration was for shit, and I just wanted to go back home.

Wilkes wrote on his notepad for a long stretch where I did my best to focus on his pencil holder, and then he cleared his throat. "And where is Dr. Morganstern now?"

"He's gone."

"For good? Or is he going to haunt the broom closet?"

I narrowed my eyes. I suspected Wilkes was mocking me now that he had his statement in place, but maybe not. Maybe he was just curious. He was so deadpan, it was difficult to tell. Crash would probably know. Empathy and all that. Crash also would've probably spit on Wilkes by now and then called him a pig.

"I think Morganstern's work is done and he's moving on."

"Mm hm. Suppose Officer Burke cuts some kind of deal with the Feds and gets himself a break? What then? Can the doctor come back?"

I had no idea what Wilkes was getting at. "I guess it's a possibility."

"So what's to keep people in the Great Beyond if there's a revolving door that'll just let them come and go however they please?"

If Wilkes and I were friends batting ideas back and forth over coffee, I wouldn't have minded the question. But we weren't friends. And I was fairly sure he was mocking me now. Jackass.

I sighed and reminded myself that people make fun of things they don't understand. Maybe Wilkes really did think he'd have Morganstern moaning and rattling chains right down the hall, and he was saving face by acting like a tough guy. I glanced up at the ceiling in the corner of the room that I'd avoided looking at throughout our interview. A taut rope that came from nowhere swayed gently, with a hanged body twitching in its noose. The ghost's feet danced just over the corners of Wilkes' desk, one in a worn-down cowboy boot, the other in a holey gray sock.

"I dunno." I cut my eyes away from the bloated rigor of the ghost's face. "I guess that when they're good and dead, they stay that way." I started humming to myself to drown out the noise of the creaking rope while Wilkes finished dotting his i's and crossing his t's.

Maurice let me finish my cold medicine and doze, off and on, all the way back to Chicago. We'd been at the sheriff's department practically another whole day, and thankfully the Feds agreed to meet with us on our home turf. I considered us lucky to be able to get back home. If the Feds wanted to pull rank, they could easily have forced us to stay in the boonies. But Maurice and I were credible enough, at least to people who didn't really know us, and I imagined their agents would rather get a nice hotel room on Michigan Avenue than stay at some truck stop off Route 66.

My phone died around the fiftieth time I called Jacob just to say hello. I missed him something fierce, and I needed to look into his eyes while he reassured me that he hadn't left me. But it was probably just as well that my cell phone crapped out. I was starting to sound like a babbling idiot.

I was sleeping pretty well, given the cockeyed angle of my neck, when Maurice rested his hand on my shoulder. "Victor. We're here."

Early morning sunlight slanted through the gaps in the apartment buildings. It was my street, but it looked strange somehow. Not quite real. Jackie the Prostitute was nowhere to be seen, but maybe I couldn't count on getting a visual on her anymore, not without the spiked doses of Starbucks. And my sinuses were so bone-dry I was pretty sure the cold medicine was still in effect, too.

Maurice looped his arm through mine, once he hauled me out of the car. I batted at him since I could walk by myself—probably—but he ignored it. I decided it was easier to just lean on him and let him deal with the rusty courtyard gate.

"You're gonna stay with me, right?" I asked as Maurice helped me up the three flights of stairs to my apartment. They seemed narrower and dingier than I'd noticed before.

"I got you home, didn't I?"

He took the keys out of my jacket pocket and tried them, one after another, in my lock. He was squinting at them and trying to figure out which one to try next when the lock tumbled and my front door opened in. Jacob had flown to California and back, and somehow managed to make it home before me. He grabbed me, and pulled me to him. "Thank you," he said to Maurice.

Jacob. I hugged him, hard. My street, my building, nothing seemed exactly like I'd remembered it. Except for Jacob. Jacob felt real.

"You still want me to stay with you?" Maurice said. Even though my face was pressed into Jacob's chest and I couldn't see Maurice, I could tell he was smiling. "I'm gonna head on home and catch up on a little shuteye."

My apartment looked familiar, small and trashy and white, as usual. I made the rounds anyway, peeking in cabinets and drawers and checking the TV to make sure I didn't have any unwanted visitors. Jacob leaned on the doorjamb between the kitchen and living room while I scrutinized all the static channels between the real channels by jabbing compulsively at the remote.

"Don't you think you'd better just come to bed?"

I looked at him. "How can you say that? Hugo Cooper's floating around here somewhere, just waiting for us both to go to sleep so he can get inside me and take another stab at you."

Jacob crossed his arms and looked massive. "I'm not going to let some dead murderer control where I can and can't sleep."

"Jacob...."

He crossed the room and pressed his finger to my lips. "He was only able to use you while you were on those psyactives. Take your Auracel and he won't bother us. Lisa said so."

I pushed past Jacob and went to my medicine cabinet. There were two Auracels left. Combined with the cold medicine I'd taken, one should get me through the night. I could go into The Clinic the next day and talk somebody there into giving me a refill. I doubted they'd have any objection since the new doctor they'd hired had fucking kidnapped me.

I tried not to dwell on the thought of having to start with another new doctor after all these years. And not let Jacob see me all bleary-eyed at the idea that I'd never again see Morganstern in a new and even more atrocious sweater vest.

I swallowed one Auracel and washed it down with a palmful of tap water. Jacob had resumed his man mountain pose behind me in the bathroom doorway. "How can you be so calm?" I asked him. "I had the Criss Cross Killer inside me."

"Evidently he'd been following me, since I was his arresting officer." Jacob shrugged. "I'm sure he would've loved to get inside me if he could, but I guess being a Stiff has its advantages. I had a shaman at PsyTrain smudge me before I left. He says it'll help. That, and time."

"They've got shamans at PsyTrain?" I said lamely. Jacob wedged himself past me and turned the shower on. The pattering of water on porcelain was soothing and familiar, and the tiny bathroom soon filled with steam.

Jacob stripped, and though I could pick out the X I'd carved into his chest, it wasn't as distinct as it might've been if it weren't for his chest hair. I let him pull my T-shirt over my head and unzip my jeans. I toed off my sneakers and stepped out of my clothes, and Jacob guided me into the shower.

He squeezed a shot of musk body wash into his palm and ran it down my chest. I leaned into the feel of his hands, so strong and sure, so safe. I thought he'd been leaving me, and all the while he was getting himself over to PsyTrain and talking his way in to see Lisa. I probably should've just trusted him. Maybe I did. Maybe it was me that I couldn't trust.

Jacob's hand slipped between my thighs, wet and slick, while the water sprayed against the back of my head and lulled me into my familiar Auracel daze. I wondered if I was ever totally present for Jacob, or if he always had to search for the real me between the cracks of all the drugs I took.

"It's okay," he said, with that non-psychic empathy of his, and he slid his palm around enough to make a lather.

I sighed and propped my shoulder against the shower wall.

His hands moved over my hips and met again on my ass, kneading me, teasing me with a soapy finger. I pressed my forehead into his shoulder and tried to stop worrying. My cock had already been convinced that everything was hunky-dory. It was poking Jacob in the thigh, stiff and ready.

Jacob turned his head so that his lips grazed my ear. "You don't have to channel anyone unless you want to," he said, low and close.

I shuddered and slipped a hand around his waist, and pressed myself against him tighter. I was just fine with never having someone else's ghost inside me again. Ever.

"You should take some time off. A big block of time. Rest. Take a vacation." His index finger slid into me while he talked, and his voice was gentle and hypnotic. I gasped and bit on his shoulder, working gently with my teeth as that finger of his moved in and out.

"You like playing with my ass," I whispered. Too porno for my taste, but I was going somewhere with it.

"Mm hm," he murmured, and his finger sank in deeper. His big cock was hard now, too, brushing against my stomach.

I smeared some of the body wash off my chest and grabbed him by the cock with a soap-slick hand. He gasped and his head fell back, eyes closed, lips parted. I gave him a few good strokes, then turned myself around and ground my backside against him. "Take it, then."

He ran his hands down my back, sliding his hot, wet cock experimentally along my ass crack.

"Come on," I prompted. Just me, Jacob, and some body wash. Because all the talk about not having any condoms around had only been an excuse. We get blood tests quarterly on the force; all the cops do, even the elite ones like us. I'd just been a little leery about letting him in. Figuratively and literally.

Another squirt of body wash ran down my back, and Jacob's hands followed. He smoothed the slickness over my skin. His palms glided over my spine and ribs, working up a lather. He pushed his soapy fingers into my ass again, and he sucked his breath in hard as he did it.

I got my feet planted and tried not to hurry him. I thought he'd probably wanted to just throw me down and fuck me for so long that he needed to savor the moment now. It felt amazing to be wanted like that. I wiped a trace of soap from my chest and grabbed my own cock, stroking it slowly.

Something pressed against my ass that was definitely not a finger. I let my breath out and rocked back, hungry for the moment that its girth would fill me up. Jacob murmured a stream of encouragement, "Oh God, oh yeah…" that turned into a more primal, wordless sound as he pushed in. A shallow thrust, and another, and then he pressed in—deep.

I let my breath out as he clasped me against him with his cock buried to the root. It hurt, and it was awesome. Eventually I'd adjust to having a boyfriend who was hung like that, but for now it was practically like getting my cherry popped all over again.

A whimpery noise escaped me, and Jacob's slick hands raked over my chest. He found a nipple and tweaked it hard. He pulled out and pushed in again, and my cock felt deliciously, painfully stiff. I had to stop stroking it and just hold myself up as Jacob started to move, my ass just barely stretching around him.

"Uhnn, God," I finally said. My forehead mashed against the shower wall as his thrusts turned into a steady pounding, and his fingertips left stinging trails behind as he struggled to grip me but couldn't quite do it because of the slipperiness of the soap. Jacob made an inarticulate noise in reply and finally got one arm around my waist, while his other hand groped my balls and cock.

I pressed my palms flat against the shower wall and pushed back, slamming onto his cock as hard as the slippery, sloppy shower would allow. The sound of his wet balls slapping against my ass rang loud in the hard-walled enclosure, and I could hear it even over the steady hiss and patter of the water. His arm was so tight around my middle I could hardly breathe, and his hand pulled my cock in time with every hard, deep thrust.

It got so intense that I stopped caring if we'd fall. I gave up trying to hold onto anything and stopped pushing back at Jacob. I let him take over and hold us both up. He fucked me so hard he'd started lifting me off the floor of the tub, and the pulse in my cock thrummed in time with the rhythm of his thrusts.

My come shot out in a brief arc that was battered away in the spray of the shower. I moaned out loud, and water filled my eyes and mouth as my head lolled back. There was a moment that seemed to extend as Jacob held me there, both of my feet off the shower floor, as my ass throbbed, and another spurt of mine shot its way into the stream.

Jacob grunted and slammed me onto him again, and once more, and then the sensation of heat welled inside my ass, and everything turned slick.

His giant cock was still inside me. He eased me back down and pushed into me a few more times. His strokes were slick with come, just a few more gentle thrusts before he softened. He let go of my waist and ran his hands down my back again, muttering things to himself that were pretty much lost to the sound of the shower. Mostly my name.

He pressed his chest to my back and I sagged into the shower wall. His lips slid on the back of my neck, wet kisses, and he cupped his hand protectively over my spent cock.

Jacob was still asleep when I woke up again, mid-morning the next day. He had this way of lying diagonally on the bed so that when I got up and looked back at him, I wondered how the hell I'd even fit in there. I crept from the bedroom and eased the door shut behind me, hoping to buy him a little more well-earned sleep.

Channel 8 was its usual non-self. I watched it carefully at first, sneaking small glances to see if there were any faces there, any grasping hands. But there weren't; it was just dirty gray snow. The single Auracel I'd taken had worn off. It was such a small dose it hadn't even left me with its characteristic behind-the-eye hangover. My tongue felt a little wooly from the cold medicine, but aside from that, I was clear.

I stared at my set and thought about the television in the hotel room. Most of the actual television components had probably been gutted, since it didn't even really function as a TV. Maybe it was all just a prop, a screen and a DVD player slapped onto the front to camouflage a big hunk of equipment that generated heat and a little electronic hum. Or maybe parts of it were actually once a TV, in another life.

If I could get my hands on one of those, I could stop getting stressed out about Jackie the Hooker, the baby in the basement, and the hovering, greedy spirit of the Criss Cross Killer. I could figure out what those dials and knobs meant and totally fine-tune it. I could blow off my appointments at The Clinic and not need to worry about running out of Auracel. If the device was portable, I could take it to crime scenes and amp up the spirits that were faint, or reluctant, or just plain old.

Who was I kidding? It was unlikely I'd use it for work; I just wanted to come home to a little peace.

Crash was the only person I could think of to help me figure out what that souped-up television was so that I could get one for myself. My heart didn't palpitate at the mere thought of him anymore, and I was glad. It didn't seem like Jacob would decide I was a little too uptight for his taste and go back to someone who knew a few more tricks in bed, not after all we'd been through. And I was faithful, too, if only in my waking life. If Jacob was gonna go out for that metaphorical pack of smokes, I suspected he would have done it by now.

The hardwood floor creaked. I looked up and Jacob was standing in the bedroom doorway, arms crossed over his chest, watching me watch Channel 8. I raised my eyebrows and waited for him to say something, but he just gave me a slow, wolfish smile.

I wondered if the invitation to move in together was still on the table. Not that I was ready to give it any serious consideration just yet, but it was comforting to know that Jacob would take things to the next level, if I was game. I'd need to have my own room—white, of course. But then he could get his dining room table back.

I bet Jacob owned a piece of shelving that'd be just right for one of those kick-ass GhosTVs.

About This Story

Funny to think Crash didn't appear until Criss Cross. I suppose I didn't need him until it was time to expand on Jacob's history. Now he's become a prominent secondary character in the series, but I knew he was special from the minute he strode onto the page. He started his life as the protagonist's obnoxious younger brother in a novel that will never see the light of day, because I firmly believe that every writer has a few stinky novels in them that just need to be written and then hidden away, and maybe culled for good characters or plot points to adapt...and believe me, this one was thoroughly culled. Anyway, "Jimmy" (as he was called in this novel) lived with the protagonist's mentally-declining dad, and he asserted his individuality by bringing home inappropriate sex partners, having wild sex that made everyone uncomfortable, and then challenging whether his family had the right to say anything about it.

So I imagine that's where Crash's libido came from. But back when he was "Jimmy", he also had a kind of moral center that was beginning to take shape, this sense of being obnoxiously right. And that became another cornerstone of Crash's personality for me. He's someone who does things in a brutally honest way, maybe to be hurtful or maybe not, maybe because he really does just think he simply calls things as he sees them.

What's cool about the characteristic of extreme honesty was that it made him a natural choice for Carolyn's best friend...because when you think about it, it's got to be beyond exhausting to be Carolyn. And liberating to finally meet someone who's not telling little white lies all the time.

About the Author

Author and artist Jordan Castillo Price is origi-
nally from Buffalo, New York, though she's been
a Midwesterner long enough that she can pass
as a born and bred Wisconsinite. Over the years,
she's tried her hand at all sorts of creative endeav-
ors, from wildly impractical to surprisingly useful
—including art, music and design—but has found
fiction writing flows the most freely and connects
her with the greatest number of people.

In her spare time she spoils her cat, leads water
aerobics, stuffs people full of cake, and daydreams
about interesting ways in which society might
collapse.

**If you enjoyed the book, please leave a review.
Even a brief review is beneficial to the author.
It DOES make a difference!**

www.psycop.com

More Stories by Jordan